PASTORAL

ANDRÉ ALEXIS

Coach House Books, Toronto

first edition

Published with the generous assistance of the Canada Council for the Arts and the Ontario Arts Council. Coach House Books also acknowledges the support of the Government of Canada through the Canada Book Fund and the Government of Ontario through the Ontario Book Publishing Tax Credit.

LIBRARY AND ARCHIVES CANADA CATALOGUING IN PUBLICATION

Alexis, André, 1957-, author
    Pastoral / André Alexis.

Issued in print and electronic formats.
ISBN 978-1-55245-286-8 (pbk.).

    I. Title.

PS8551.L474P37 2014   c813'.54   C2013-907679-4

Pastoral is available as an ebook: ISBN 978 1 55245 370 4

Purchase of the print version of this book entitles you to a free digital copy. To claim your ebook of this title, please email sales@chbooks.com with proof of purchase or visit chbooks.com/digital. (Coach House Books reserves the right to terminate the free digital download offer at any time.)

To Jane Ruddell
and Veronika Krausas
and Roo Borson

And In Memoriam Eighteen

Only the billowing overcoat remains,
everything else is made up.
– Franz Kafka, *Diaries* (1912)

I

APRIL

Christopher Pennant had passed through a crisis of faith. His
time at seminary had not been enough to free him entirely
from doubt, but it had given him the strength to go on, and when
he'd taken holy orders he had been both proud and relieved.

While waiting for a parish of his own, he assisted Father Scarduto
at St. Matthew's, in Ottawa. This suited Christopher perfectly. He
was himself from Ottawa, so some of the strangeness (and pleasure)
of being called 'Father Pennant' was offset by the familiarity of his
surroundings. Whenever he allowed himself to think about where
he might like to go – that is, where he might like his first parish to be
– he imagined he'd be happiest in a small city of some sort:
Cambridge, say, or Peterborough. So, he was dismayed when he was
told he'd be going to a place in Lambton County called Barrow.

He was not unhappy to be leaving the city, but the city was
where he had lived out most of his life and the word 'country' –
Barrow was in the 'country' – was vague to him. It was a word that
called to mind Cumberland, the town near which his parents had a

cottage, the place where he'd spent his summers as a child. He had vivid memories of its farm fields and hills, but he had never gotten to know the town itself or its inhabitants. So, Barrow would be an adventure. He hoped he would be a suitable shepherd for those who needed spiritual guidance.

It would be fair to add that there was a hint of condescension to Father Pennant's attitude. He assumed that the 'country' was simpler than the city, that rural routes were, metaphorically speaking, straighter than metropolitan ones. It followed, in his mind, that the people of Barrow would be more straightforward than those who lived in and around the Byward Market.

That this was not true he learned almost at once.

Barrow was a town of 1,100 inhabitants. Whether through some divine compulsion for equilibrium or through poor census taking, its population had been 1,100 for twenty years. In every other way, Barrow was a typical town in Ontario, with its grocery store, greasy spoon and churches.

Just outside of Barrow – and all around it – there were fields, silos, barns and farmhouses. Coming in by bus, Father Pennant was so enchanted by the land, by the thistles and yellowish reeds at the side of the road, that he asked the driver to let him off at the sign that said 'Welcome to Barrow' so he could walk into town, suitcase and all, on the warm April day that was his first in his new parish.

It was a Monday morning. There were few people about, few distractions. So, Father Pennant easily took in the trees, the birdsong, the crocuses along the sidewalk and the sky-mirroring ditch water that gently rippled when the wind blew.

As he walked along Main Street, a shop door opened beside him. The smell of bread saturated the air and a man came out with an apron full of crusts and crumbs. He shook his apron. The bits of bread fell onto the street and, from nowhere, a dozen pigeons descended, their wings flapping, quivering, flapping.

Turning to the priest, the man said

– Morning. John Harrington

and held out his hand.

– Good morning, answered Father Pennant.

The priest was just under six feet, dark-skinned, neither fat nor thin, brown-eyed and handsome. He wore a black jacket, black pants, a black shirt with a clerical collar and, on top of it all, a dark overcoat. Mr. Harrington smiled.

– Nice day, eh, Father? Would you like a kaiser roll or ... No, wait. I have just the thing.

Before Father Pennant could speak, Mr. Harrington went into the bakery and emerged with a loaf of bread: warm, dark, somewhat round, pockmarked, smelling of yeast, molasses and burnt walnuts.

– Thank you so much, said Father Pennant.

He was about to walk on, pleased with his gift, when the baker said

– That'll be two-fifty, Father.

As Father Pennant, startled and slightly embarrassed by the misunderstanding, reached into his pocket for the money, a ginger-coloured mutt charged at the pigeons. The dog was so obviously playing, however, that the pigeons scarcely moved out of its way. They turned their backs to it and went on pecking, as if it were common knowledge that the worst this mutt could do was wet them with its tongue.

– Bruno, called Mr. Harrington, leave the pigeons alone.

The dog barked, as if to say

– Yes, all right

then left the pigeons alone, bounding away as suddenly as he'd jumped among them.

Father Pennant's first view of St. Mary's church was gratifying. The church was plain, not at all grandiose, though its stained-glass windows, lit up by the afternoon sun, were a little garish. The rectory beside it was also plain. It was two storeys high, narrow, and had grey stone walls and a black-shingled roof. A young maple tree stood on its front lawn. The house was, or at least looked to be, perfect for him.

As he approached, Father Pennant noticed two older men sitting in wicker chairs on the porch. The men were partially obscured by shadow. One of them rose to greet him and Father Pennant saw that he was not as old as all that. His hair was white. He was gaunt. He needed a shave, and his bright blue sweater was fuzzy and frayed. But when he shook Father Pennant's hand, his grip was firm. And his voice was strong and clear. He was in his late fifties, early sixties perhaps.

– Father, he said. I'm Lowther Williams.

Then, with a movement of his head toward the shade-hidden man behind him

– That's my friend, Heath Lambert.

– Are you the caretaker? asked Father Pennant.

– If you like. I don't think of myself that way, though. For Father Fowler, I did the cooking and cleaning and just about everything he couldn't do for himself.

– I'm sorry, I thought there was a woman who did the cooking and cleaning. Someone from the parish.

– There was Mrs. Young, but she died two years ago, and I kind of took up the slack.

– I see. That's great, but I'll have to ask the bishop. We don't have ... I don't think we can afford ...

– You don't have to worry about the money, Father. I had an agreement with Father Fowler. I work for room and board and a few dollars now and then. If it's okay with you, I'd like to carry on.

– I think I'll still have to check with the bishop. I'm a pretty good cook myself and I like to keep things tidy, so I don't know if I'll need anyone seven days a week. But let me talk it over with the bishop. You can stay on till then.

– No, said Lowther. I don't think that would be right. I won't stay if you've got no use for me. You can call me if you need anything fixed or anything. I'll be at my mother's old house in Petrolia for a while. The number's in the parish phone book, by the phone.

Behind them, Heath Lambert rose from his chair and came down from the porch.

– I told you, he said softly to Lowther.

Feeling as if he'd been unpleasant, Father Pennant relented at once.

– No, no, he said. On second thought, I'm wrong. I'll need someone for the first few weeks at least, until I get on my feet. If you don't mind, I'll still check with Bishop Henry, but it'd be great if you stayed on for a bit. Is that okay?

Heath and Lowther looked at him as if they were amused.

– Yes, said Lowther. Thank you, Father.

They shook hands. Or, rather, Lowther took the loaf of bread from Father Pennant and *then* they shook hands. Lowther then withdrew, speaking softly with Heath who, after a moment, walked off, raising his hand in a wave meant for the two behind him.

Lowther opened the door to the rectory. The house was filled with light. There was a window in every wall. There was very little furniture: a chair and chesterfield in the living room, table and chairs in the dining room, a kitchen with a white linoleum floor, a white stove, a white fridge, light green cupboards. Everything was spotless. By the looks of it, Lowther Williams was a tidy and thorough housekeeper. Upstairs was much the same. Father Pennant's bedroom had a small closet, a severe, Shaker-style bed and an equally severe bedside table on which stood a round-bodied, white-hooded lamp. His bedroom window looked down onto the maple on the lawn and over at the yard of St. Mary's school. Lowther's room, at the back of the house, was as bright as Father Pennant's and as chaste. But there was a music stand in the room, and on the stand a score stood open. Beside the stand, a cello lay on its side.

– I hope you don't mind, Father, said Lowther. I've been playing since I was twelve.

– I don't mind at all, said Father Pennant.

From the rectory, Father Pennant and Lowther went into the church. St. Mary's was tall-ceilinged but relatively small. There was a nave, but it was barely deep enough to accommodate the font, a shallow but wide white porcelain bowl set on a solid rectangle of dark wood. There were two rows of ten pews, enough room for two or three hundred parishioners. The pews were of an unstained wood that had been lacquered and looked almost ochre. Though the lights in the church were off, its interior had the warm feeling of a gallery or museum. The church's four stained-glass windows were its first oddity. The windows depicted moments in the lives of rather obscure saints. On the left, if one were facing the altar, were Abbo of Fleury, shown being killed by rioters, and Alexis of Rome, dressed as a beggar with a book. On the right were Zenobius of Florence, depicted helping a man rise from a coffin, and St. Zeno, shown laughing at the side of a lake, a fish in his hand.

– Why these particular saints? asked Father Pennant.

– Father Fowler's predecessor wanted two A's and two Z's, answered Lowther. He thought it would remind people just how many saints there have been and maybe encourage them to be saintly themselves.

– Hmm, said Father Pennant.

He would have preferred more recognizable figures (St. Paul or St. Anthony, say), but the four obscure saints did not diminish his liking for the church. If anything, he was, when he thought about it, inclined to agree with his predecessor. There was something about these little-known saints that suggested the great range of sanctity.

The church's second oddity was endearing. In the sacristy just off from the altar there were the usual things (vestments, wine, unconsecrated hosts) as well as a surprising number of candles. It was as if Father Fowler had feared a shortage of wax. There were dozens of candles – tall, short, narrow, thick, round, hexagonal – neatly stacked on the floor and in the cupboards and cabinets. The sacristy itself smelled of candle wax.

Father Pennant had assumed the church would be eccentric, something amusing to talk about when he visited the bishop or wrote to his fellow priests. Small-town churches were almost always eccentric. But here was a church in his own image: modest and straightforward, despite its oddities. It might be that his parishioners were 'prickly,' as he'd been warned, but his church and rectory were all he might have wished for.

The rest of Father Pennant's first day in Barrow was uneventful. He unpacked his clothes and put them in the chest of drawers in his closet. He inspected the books Father Fowler had left on the book-shelves: novels, mostly. He ate the first meal Lowther prepared for him: trout with lemon and salt. The trout, perfectly cooked, lay headless on a bed of white rice beside a small handful of fried mush-rooms. And for dessert, apple-ginger crumble.

To think he had almost dismissed Lowther before tasting the man's cooking! But then, Lowther was not easy to gauge. He had appeared to be an old man, but he was, in fact, only sixty-two. He seemed to be rudderless, but he was self-assured and spiritually oriented. He treated his duties as caretaker with the utmost serious-ness, but when Father Pennant asked him why he chose to be the parish's caretaker, Lowther answered that there was no particular reason. It was the same answer he gave when asked about the cello: no particular reason. The cello had belonged to his grandfather. Asked by his mother if he would like to play the cello, he had answered yes, though he had felt neither compelled nor all that interested. Once he chose a thing, however, Lowther devoted himself to it completely. To Father Pennant, there seemed something almost superstitious about the strength of Lowther's devotions.

– Do you believe in God? Father Pennant casually asked.

– Yes, very much, answered Lowther.

Which was good enough for Father Pennant who, reassured, spent the rest of the evening reading *Memoirs of a Midget* (a novel he chose for its unusual title) before falling asleep in his room, his sleep haunted by passages from Debussy's *Sonata for Cello*.

At least part of the reason for Father Pennant's enchantment with Barrow was that, without being aware of the extent of his distaste,

Christopher Pennant had tired of big cities. Ottawa, his home, had become impersonal and oppressive to him. It made him lonely just thinking about all that tar and concrete. The only things he missed about Ottawa, now that it was behind him, were its many old churches and its river, which, at least in his imagination, had constantly promised elsewhere.

This longing for 'elsewhere' had been a long time coming. Christopher Pennant had always imagined that the city would be the place he'd be most needed. After seminary he had devoted himself to those whom the city had decimated: the poor, the addicted, the downtrodden. And he had felt his work was necessary. But that which had driven him to the priesthood in the first place, the spiritual presence of God, had grown more faint. It wasn't that Ottawa itself was godless. It was, he imagined, that any place that covered the earth with tar and concrete was a place where His presence was bound to be muted. And Father Pennant had come to resent this mutedness. He'd begun to suffer from it. So, when the parish in Barrow was offered to him, Father Pennant, though he might have preferred a smaller city to the country, hoped that southern Ontario would be a way back to the feeling of closeness with God, a way back to the fount of his own spirituality.

His first moments in Barrow were enchanting because they suggested that his hopes were not misplaced. The dun hay that covered the fields like rotting mats, the crocuses, chicory and dandelions, the songs of the birds, the clouds so solid and white it was as if they were being held up from below: everything brought relief and joy. These feelings in turn brought him a kind of grateful curiosity about the town itself and he tried to learn as much as he could about Barrow and the land around it.

Founded in 1904 by an oil baron named Richmond Barrow, the town was, originally, a settlement for those who worked in the oil fields of Lambton County. Over the decades its importance had receded with the oil, but as Barrow was not far from Sarnia it became something of a suburb: near enough by car but still far enough away to maintain its independence and personality.

Along with its history, Barrow also had its mysteries. First among them was its haunted house. Barrow Mansion, the oldest house in town, had been the site of two murders. During the first, Richmond Barrow was stabbed to death by his wife, the former Eleanor Miller of Oil Springs. Years later, Richmond's son, Clive, was stabbed by *his* wife, the former Eleanor Burgin of Strathroy. After a century, the two deaths merged in the minds of the town's inhabitants, some forgetting that *two* Barrows had been murdered, though there was general agreement that the name 'Eleanor' was a bad omen and that the mansion was haunted.

The first sightings of the town's ghosts came shortly after Barrow Mansion had been turned into a museum, in the 1950s. After that it was easy to find men and women who swore they had seen 'Mr. Barrow' wandering the mansion's corridors. By all accounts, the ghost was as baffled as the townspeople. It sometimes wandered the mansion with (according to witnesses) a knife or a fork or garden shears protruding from its chest. These ghostly apparitions were traumatic for those who experienced them, but they were a boon to the town itself: the mansion attracted the curious and the skeptical, all of whom came from places like Wallaceburg or Timiskaming or even Saskatoon to see the house and its spectral occupants for themselves

No doubt, Barrow's reputation for 'prickliness' came with its ghosts. The people of Barrow, most of whom were of English stock, were neither gregarious like hard-oilers from Petrolia nor voluble, like the inhabitants of Bright's Grove. They were quiet, not much given to talking with strangers. They were not unfriendly to those who came to see the mansion, but they were cautious and their caution was taken, by those who'd come to see the ghosts, for 'attitude.' And yet the townspeople were capable of great warmth and generosity. On Barrow Day, for instance.

Barrow Day was a celebration of the town's founding. All visitors were welcome. The day began with masses said in the town's churches. Then there was a parade, a banquet and, finally, a fête in a gravel pit to mark the end of the festivities. Those who found themselves in

Barrow on June 15 were almost inevitably overwhelmed by the generosity, passion and drunkenness of the townspeople. On Barrow Day, when something of Barrow's 'earth spirit' surfaced, the town's mood belied its reputation for reticence and reserve.

Barrow Mansion and Barrow Day were two of the town's mysteries. There is a third, but one can't talk about Barrow without first mentioning an aspect of the town that is less than mysterious but that was, for Father Pennant, just as affecting as ghosts and parades. That is, the physical beauty of the land on which Barrow lay.

Barrow was the quintessence of southern Ontario: low hills, thick scrubby woods, farm fields sprouting corn or grain, grey barns, farmhouses, maples, elms, weeping willows, apple orchards, the dark brown earth, alfalfa for the cows, acres of grazing land for sheep or horses; the smell of it: sweet, acrid, nasty, vegetal; robins, blue jays, scarlet tanagers, cardinals, hummingbirds; thistles, pussy willow, clover, Queen Anne's lace, dandelions.

The land around Barrow was that aspect of the world one would willingly worship, if one were a pantheist, say, or a pagan, as opposed to a priest.

On his second day in Barrow, Father Pennant rose at five. Lowther had been awake for some time and had prepared a breakfast of apple-cinnamon pancakes with back bacon. He had grated the apple himself and had timed it so that the bacon was hot when Father Pennant sat down, but there was little sign that the kitchen had been used. Everything had been cleaned up by the time Father Pennant ate and, shortly after he finished, it would have been difficult to show he had eaten at all. His dishes had been washed, dried and put away.

The early service was well-attended that morning. There were at least twenty-five people at the low mass, most of whom came to get a look at the new priest.

After the mass, few stayed to talk. Those who did did not stay long. The day and the world called. But Father Pennant had the impression he'd been deemed acceptable. No one had been unfriendly or dubious or overtly critical. He had made a good beginning, surely. But just to be certain, Father Pennant spoke to Lowther, who'd attended.

– How was it?

– It was good, answered Lowther. Your voice doesn't shake as much as Father Fowler's.

– That's not a ringing endorsement, Lowther.

– No, Father, but this was low mass. It'll be different when you sing.

There were a number of visitors to the rectory that day. It was sunny and warm. You could feel summer approach. Which, perhaps, explains why two women brought mounds of Jell-O in which the preserved remains of the previous summer's strawberries and raspberries were suspended. Another parishioner brought cherry pie and an angel food cake so airy it clung to Father Pennant's front teeth as soon as he bit it. There were plans for an official welcome. It was to take place the following Sunday. But those who came to the rectory on Father Pennant's second day were the ones who could not resist seeing him sooner. Here was the man to whom they would confess the darkest things. It was important to feel him out. Mrs. Young, for instance, after she had watched him eat a piece of her macaroni pie, quietly asked what he thought of adultery.

– It's a sin, answered Father Pennant.

– Yes, but I wonder where it is on the scale of things. Is it worse than murder?

– No, said Father Pennant, but all our sins are interconnected. One is the road to another.

– I never thought of it that way, said Mrs. Young. I'll be sure to tell that husband of mine what you said.

Then, looking at him meaningfully, she asked

– Did you like the macaroni pie? It's my mother's recipe.

The morning was busy and then, following the afternoon mass, there were even more people to meet, more food to sample: a pear cake, a honey and plum cobbler, an apple crumble. In a matter of hours, Father Pennant had a strong sense of his parish. It was as normal as could be. And here again, he felt fortunate. It would be a pleasure getting to know those who'd been too shy or too busy to approach him early on.

The day's only sour note came from an old woman named Tomasine Humble. Her hands constricted by arthritis, her thin body like a knotty stick under a thick yellow dress, her white hair held stiffly in place by hairspray, she was not in a good mood, or perhaps she was in the best mood her ailments permitted. When someone asked if Father Pennant had enjoyed a piece of cake, he'd answered

– Yes, very much.

But Tomasine had muttered

– Not on your life.

and smiled when he looked at her inquisitively.

When someone else mentioned the good weather they'd been having, Father Pennant answered that he was looking forward to exploring the countryside in spring, to watching the gardens bloom. Tomasine Humble then said

– Not much point in that. You should be taking care of souls, not gardens.

– I can do both, surely, Mrs. Humble.

– We don't know what you can do at all, she'd answered.

– Well, I hope I won't disappoint you.

– You'll disappoint me. There hasn't been a priest yet who hasn't disappointed me.

– Perhaps I'll disappoint you less?

– I live in hope, young man.

With that, she had turned away, her point made, apparently.

Despite Mrs. Humble's warning that the soul, not the earth, was his proper domain, Father Pennant spent the last hours of his first afternoon exploring the countryside around Barrow. He was driven about in an old Volkswagen by Lowther, who also acted as his guide. Everywhere the earth was coming back to life: here, a scarlet tanager, like a tongue of flame, alighted on a telephone wire; there, at their feet, a shrew scampered for cover. The earth, which has only two words, intoned the first of them ('life') noisily, with birdsong, the gurgle and slap of rushing water, the suck and squelch of the ground itself. Not that its other word ('death') was banished. As they walked in a field, Father Pennant spotted a small clearing over which bleached animal bones (ribs, skulls, backbones and limbs) were strewn. Among and through the bones, young grass grew. It was like an open ossuary.

– What's this? asked Father Pennant.

– I'm not sure, said Lowther. Maybe someone dumped the remains of animals they didn't mean to trap. Poachers, most likely.

The most impressive thing they saw that afternoon, however, came as they stood by George Bigland's farm admiring the violets and thistle. They were on their side of the barbed wire when Father Pennant saw, in the distance, a dark sheep. It was followed by others and still others until, after a while, it was as if a wave of sheep, baaing and crying out, were subsiding in their direction. The sheep, their fleeces dark with dirt, seemed aware of Father Pennant's and Lowther's presences. They pooled about on the other side of the fence, hundreds of them. Then, curiosity satisfied, they dispersed, going off here and there to eat the short grass.

Lowther was an ideal guide to the fields. He knew the names of all the birds, grasses and wildflowers. As Father Pennant was himself an amateur naturalist, his respect for Lowther grew. It grew immea surably when he discovered the sheer breadth of Lowther's learning. Lowther seemed to have read everything and his memory was extraordinary. He could, if asked, recite reams of Coleridge and Shakespeare, Dante and Hopkins. He was modest and self-effacing, but there was also something slightly disturbing about him. Why should such an evidently talented man be satisfied working at the rectory? How did he support himself? What was he after, exactly? It troubled Father Pennant to think this way about a man with whom he felt a kinship, but it was like finding a gold ring in a back garden: you had to wonder to whom it belonged.

Then, too, there was the angularity of Lowther's thinking. As they were driving to Petrolia and talking about southern Ontario, it emerged that Lowther did not like to speak of the past. He insisted that what had been was a distraction from the here and now. To Father Pennant, this seemed a clear contradiction. The past was the place from which Coleridge and Hopkins reached us, no? Lowther was steeped in the past, wasn't he?

– You must be right, Father, but I don't think of it that way. A tea bag comes from somewhere, but tea exists when you pour hot water on it. I'm steeped in the *present*.

– Yes, but what about tradition and the people who came before us? You and I wouldn't be here, we wouldn't be talking, if it weren't for what came before us.

– I'm sure you're right, Father, but I don't see the contradiction. The past has no meaning, absolutely none.

– Hmmm ...

As they drove over the dirt roads and along narrow lanes, stopping now and then to admire a farmhouse or a striking vista, it seemed to Father Pennant that his companion was trustworthy, more or less, but Lowther Williams was also difficult to read.

Anne Young, who had asked Father Pennant about the relative weight of adultery, was not afraid her husband had been unfaithful. For one thing, John Young was as lazy a man as she could imagine. Though he was still handsome and desirable at sixty, he was not the kind of man to take on the work of planning, calculating and deceiving. He might commit adultery, but only if there were very little movement involved. Besides, he loved her, and she was sure of it. They had gone through so much together: childlessness, hard times, deaths and, most importantly, the adoption of his sister's daughter, Elizabeth. In these crises he had been all that one could have wanted from a husband. And loving him the way she did, there was no question *she* would be unfaithful. He was the only man she had ever slept with. Not that she hadn't been curious, from time to time, but she was curious about all sorts of things and you would no more find her with another man than you would have found her drinking a glass of Cynar, that greenish, artichoke liqueur her neighbours had brought back from Italy.

Adultery was on her mind, though, because she had seen Robbie Myers with Jane Richardson, and Robbie Myers was her niece Elizabeth's fiancé. If he was not, technically speaking, 'adulterous,' there was almost certainly a serious name for his behaviour.

Elizabeth had come to stay with them under the worst circumstances. She was the daughter of John's sister, Eileen, and one summer, seventeen years ago now, Eileen had asked if they would mind taking care of Liz while she and her husband went off to Europe for a romantic holiday. Childless themselves, Anne and John adored children, so they had happily accepted. But Elizabeth's parents had drowned when their ferry sank somewhere between Piraeus and Naxos. It was a tragedy on a number of fronts. John was, of course, devastated by the death of his younger sister and her husband. And then she and John were bewildered to find themselves entangled in legal proceedings to determine who should take care of the child. And then there was the three-year-old Liz, a strange little puzzle. They did not at first know how to tell her that her parents had died, but when they did tell her, it was as if the child could not or would not understand. For months Liz would calmly ask after her parents, as if she were asking after clothes she'd misplaced. Reminded that they were dead, Liz would go back to her toys and remind the dolls and fuzzy bears that *their* parents had died.

— Your mother and father are dead, she would say to each of them.

For all of that, she grew up to be a normal young girl, whatever 'normal' was when it had its hair cut. A shy child, she had opened up at school, making friends easily at St. Mary's Primary School. From there, they had the usual problems with her. Liz questioned everything they did or said. For a time, she insisted they were not her parents and so had no authority over her. For a very long time, they could not get two words out of her. She would mutter at them on her way in or out of the house.

Then came Elizabeth's interest in boys. There were the 'wild years' with Michael Newsome, the 'dull years' with Matthew Kendal and now, finally, there was Robbie Myers. How grateful Anne had been that Liz had settled on a genuine country boy, one whose family owned a farm just outside of Bright's Grove.

As far as Anne was concerned, dealing with young love was the most difficult aspect of parenting. John regarded 'boys' as belonging to Elizabeth's private life and refused to get involved. (Did he even know the difference between Michael Newsome [black jacket, slicked hair] and Matthew Kendal [baseball in spring, hockey in winter]?) John was unconditionally loving, and that was fine, as far as it went, but Anne would have preferred to feel a little of his steadying hand where Liz's boyfriends were concerned.

Anne herself was too involved, albeit discreetly, to be impartial. She identified with Liz. She worried Liz would misstep, would end up with a good-for-nothing townie who'd waste his life drawing a paycheque from Dow Chemical and pissing it away at the Blackhawk Tavern. She wanted more for Liz whom, after all, she really did think of (and love) as a daughter. If it came to that, it sometimes seemed to Anne that Liz's relationships were more important to her than they were to Liz herself.

Despite her better instincts, despite John's sombre advice, Anne had, in the past, allowed herself to feel for this or that boy. It had broken her heart, for instance, when she learned how unfair Liz had been to young Matthew. But then, who had asked her to talk about *her* hopes for Liz and Matthew's life together? And who knows if her enthusiasm hadn't, in the end, turned Liz against the boy? She had sworn she would not allow herself to care whom Liz brought home, had sworn to remain above it all or beyond it, as John did. So, although this business with Robbie Myers would have been difficult for anyone, it was even more so for her, because she had vowed to keep out of her niece's affairs.

But what had she seen, exactly?

She had gone to Sarnia to find cloth for the new drapes she would sew for the living room. As she sometimes did when she was in the city, she allowed herself to eat at the Lucky Dragon along the strip. It wasn't only that she liked Chinese food; it gave her an indefinable thrill to eat beef with black bean sauce in a big city. So, there she was in the Lucky Dragon, at a table by the front window, when whom should she see in the parking lot outside but Robbie Myers. Her heart lifted. She genuinely liked the boy. He got out of his truck, walked around to the other side and opened the door for … Was that Jane Richardson? Yes, Fletcher Richardson's daughter: dirty blond, thin, wearing a leather jacket two sizes too big. Thank God the two did not come into the Dragon itself. It would have been humiliating to face them. But why? What had they done? Nothing explicit or illicit, not that she had seen. But you didn't have to catch people at it to know there was something between them. It was in the way Robbie had opened the door and helped her down, the way they had walked away together. That is all she had seen. Robbie Myers had helped Jane Richardson down from the cab of his Chevy. But that was enough for an attentive person. It had occurred to her – no use denying it – to follow the two wherever it was they were off to. But she had not. Instead, she had stayed in the restaurant, unable to enjoy her food, wondering if what she had seen was innocent or not.

During the days that followed, she had been as discreet as possible. She had not spoken of what she had witnessed. She had asked only two bland questions:

– Was Robbie in Sarnia the other day, Liz?

and

– Liz, are you still friends with Jane Richardson?

There was nothing more she could do without meddling. She would have to bite her tongue and observe. It was either observe or investigate. That is, snoop. As she considered snooping a vile habit, she did not snoop.

It isn't as if Elizabeth was unaware that something lay behind her aunt's questions. They were asked in such resolutely bland tones, it had been like hearing a mortician speak. Besides, Elizabeth was sensitive to any mention of her fiancé, and though she had not thought of

Jane Richardson (Robbie's first love) in a while, hearing Jane's name brought more than an inkling of the connection between them.

Despite her aunt's careful nonchalance, Elizabeth had been spooked.

When she was thoughtful, as she often was in these months before her marriage, Elizabeth liked to walk. She walked along the fence of her uncle's sod farm, whatever the season, but in spring she was comforted by the new grass, the spluttering sprinklers and the sight of the far trees, the point at which she would usually turn back for home.

Days after her aunt questioned her about Robbie and Jane, Elizabeth went out for a long walk, taking with her the prayer book that had belonged to her parents. The book was small. As a young girl, she imagined the prayer book had been made just for her. It had been slightly larger than her palm when she was eight years old, and thick as three of her small fingers. It was bound in black leather with, embedded in its cover, a single white pearl that had, somehow and for years, resisted her efforts to dislodge it. The edges of the book's pages had been gilded and, inside, it contained hundreds of prayers, prayers for every imaginable circumstance, including one that was to be said on being captured by cannibals and another to be said before eating food 'of dubious provenance.' Not that she had ever used it for its prayers. She was not devout. Her aunt and uncle were the devoted ones. From the age at which she had first been made aware of the idea, 'God' had seemed to Elizabeth a shaky proposition. It didn't help, of course, that if He existed He had murdered her parents. But, really, there was no deep calculation, no rancour or bitterness involved. She simply was not convinced or was not yet convinced of God's existence. The prayer book was a thing she held because her parents had touched it.

The sun was out and doing its best to dry the ground. The clouds were thick and white, like gouts of clotted cream in a wide blue bowl. The earth smelled of her uncle's sod and of cow manure from the next farm over, Mr. Rubie's, from which, if the air was right, you would occasionally hear the faintest lowing, a sound that always surprised her, as Rubie's farm was acres away.

For the first while, Elizabeth thought of nothing in particular. Walking was a way to stanch thought. But she was in love and that meant, for her, that Robbie was at the tip of most of the strands within her. This was a pleasant thing. She could be with him in an instant, and the image she held of him was almost as vivid as Robbie himself. Of course, there was a difference between the man within her and the one who walked about or drove around in his father's truck. The real Robert Myers was, naturally, more desirable. His eyes were always bluer than she remembered, his lashes longer. And, of course, there were aspects of him that paled in her imagination, however she tried to keep them: the light hair below his stomach, the way his back narrowed to a groove above his buttocks. These things never failed to fascinate her, because she perpetually rediscovered them.

The Robbie within her had his charms too, however. He was made up of words, of impressions. He was a bright smile, an allusive thought, an attitude she found irresistible. At times, she was at odds with herself, missing the one while with the other, wishing he were physically gone when he was there or there when he was gone. Usually, this fracas between her Robbies lasted only a moment. But now that they were to be married, there seemed to be more serious skirmishes. Who was Robbie, really? How could she know? Was he the man with whom she wished to be married 'til death? Each of these questions was a cloud above the road to church. And now, so was the question of Jane Richardson. Where did Jane fit in all this? She had been Robbie's girlfriend ages ago, in grades 9 and 10. She no longer figured in his life, did she?

Elizabeth came to the trees at the edge of her uncle's property. Instead of turning back, she climbed over the wire fence and went into the woods. The woods were cool, as always. The tightly grouped trees were a canopy, keeping the sunlight out, preserving the last granules of frost through which the ferns and fiddleheads pushed up and unfurled. There were paths that meandered confusedly about the woods, paths made, some of them, by her younger self. Or so she liked to imagine because when she'd been a girl bent on mastering the woods, she used to stamp her feet as she walked, creating faint trails that led nowhere, trails that came to sudden stops at the foot of this spruce or that white pine. She herself was well beyond needing the trails for guidance. She could have made her way through the woods with her eyes closed, reaching the destination of her choice (the highway, Fox's farm, the quarry, 'Regina') in no time.

Elizabeth chose to walk toward Regina and it was at Regina that she first saw Father Pennant, the priest who, it seemed, would preside at her wedding.

On this, his third afternoon in Barrow, Father Pennant was on his own. Lowther Williams had gone to Wyoming to deliver a supply of unconsecrated hosts to the church there. Before going, Lowther had recommended that Father Pennant visit 'Regina,' Barrow's third mystery. Regina, source of the Thames River, was discovered in 1905 by an Englishman named John Atkinson. Regina was a vein of glass-clear fresh water that sprang from the ground, ran for six feet and returned underground. The water was cold enough to rattle teeth, in summer or winter. It ran in a narrow, stony depression that tapered at its ends so that, if your imagination was so inclined, the source of the Thames resembled a vulva, which is why Atkinson, attempting wit, named it 'Regina' to rhyme with 'vagina.' The name stuck, but it was now more often called 'the Queen' by the people of Lambton County, and it had become a kind of shrine where pregnant women – farm girls, mostly – went to pray for healthy children.

Father Pennant was unprepared for Regina's beauty. The water ran so fast and constant, it was as if it did not run at all. Regina was like a solid section of crystal. Father Pennant kneeled to touch it and was surprised when his fingers parted the cold water.

It was like this that Elizabeth saw Father Pennant for the first time, coming upon him as he withdrew his fingers from the water. Startled, she apologized.

— Oh, not at all, said Father Pennant, rising. I was just admiring the Queen. Lowther told me how lovely it is, but it's really something, especially here in the middle of nowhere.

— Yes, answered Elizabeth. Are you Father Pennant?

— Yes, I am. And you are?

— Elizabeth Denny. You met my aunt the other day. Anne Young?

— So I did. I remember. She seems like a nice woman.

They shook hands and then the two of them began walking toward the highway. Beneath the shade of the trees, neither could see the other properly, but when they came to the edge of the woods the sun was still shining and each saw the other as if for the first time. Father Pennant saw a striking young woman with light brown hair, a narrow nose, a gap between her front teeth. She was dressed in slightly baggy blue jeans, and a man's work shirt beneath which she wore a pullover with three buttons (unbuttoned) at the neck. She wore wire-rimmed glasses that distracted, somewhat, from her eyes: hazel, expressive and beautiful. As they walked and spoke, he found himself happy in her company.

Elizabeth, for her part, did not take Father Pennant quite so deeply in. He was taller than she was and his hands were large, almost ungainly, like the paws of a young dog. Much more than that she did not register. He wore the uniform of the priest: black suit with a white clerical collar. Nondescript. Still, she was not uncomfortable in his presence.

They walked in the direction of town. Elizabeth would have to turn back long before they reached Barrow some seven kilometres away, but she was happy to converse, and their talk turned quickly from the general to the specific. That is, they began to talk about marriage, Elizabeth's wedding, its arrangements, the changes marriage would bring to her life, the love she felt for her fiancé.

— Have you ever been in love? she asked.

— Yes, answered Father Pennant. I know people don't think priests live full lives, but yes, I've been in love.

– Did you … ? Have you … ? You know … If you don't mind me asking?

– I don't mind, but let me keep that to myself until we know each other better. It's very personal for me. But I have been in love and I do know what it's like to want someone.

(Father Pennant knew very well what it was like to want someone. He remembered the taste of salt, the smell of a room in Italy, the touch of a hand on his back. And at the memory, the hair on the back of his head tingled as if he had been caressed.)

– Why did you become a priest, then, Father? I'm sorry if …

– No, don't apologize. I became a priest because I thought it was my calling. It's the way I wanted to be in this world. I believe in God and I think, as a priest, I can do good.

The occasional car or truck passed as they walked along the side of the road. The air smelled of the woods (a slightly fungal exhalation) mingled with the smell of the dirt road, the smell of weeds, the smell of spring.

– People tend to focus on our vow of chastity, Father Pennant continued. And I understand, because it's an unusual choice. But it isn't as if I have had an unfortunate accident. I've chosen the life I lead. I've had to learn the discipline. And I think it's made me more sensitive to the things I've given up. But even if I've given up physical love, I haven't given up on love itself. That would be perverse. I believe love is the most powerful thing in our lives. An earthly mira-cle. It's what makes marriage so precious.

– You were in love, Father, but you weren't married. Why should marriage matter, if love is such a miracle?

– Marriage is a way of saying love exists, saying it aloud, a way of sharing the thing inside you with your community. It's an act of generosity made by two people. Maybe in the past it was about other things, but times have changed.

All of which was fine and true or fine and not true, as far as Elizabeth was concerned. Either way. She had no problem with love or marriage. Her problem, insofar as it was a problem, was with doubt and apprehension – not big feelings, small ones, but just as distracting. She would not be completely at ease until she knew what her doubts meant or how she was to take them. But she was grateful for Father Pennant's advice.

When it came time for them to part, she for home and he for town, Elizabeth thanked the priest and shook his hand again before heading off. Father Pennant smiled and said

– See you soon

before turning his attention to the walk home.

In the distance, the sun was setting. A pink tinge grew slowly more scarlet on one side of the clouds and evening insinuated itself from above, turning the upper arch of sky indigo.

II

MAY

Father Pennant's move to the country – away from civilization – was not without its inconveniences. The rectory's wiring was ancient and unpredictable. Though the freezer and stove were reliable, the lights in the house sometimes cut out without warning and returned just as unexpectedly. It would have been too expensive to have the rectory rewired, so they learned to deal with the fickle lights. Father Pennant now understood his predecessor's thing for candles. He made use of the many Father Fowler had collected. Every room in the house had its own brass candle holder and he grew accustomed to reading by candlelight, to sepia darkness punctured by candle flame.

The town took to its new priest without difficulty. Most of the Catholics in Barrow thought him likeable and sympathetic. The rest of the town treated him with the deference due a priest. So, it was not long before he felt welcome. Of course, the hallmark of welcome is being let in on gossip and, as is the case in any small town, there were innumerable rumours circulating, rumours about his parishioners and stories about people he did not know at all. The gossip Father Pennant heard most often concerned Lowther. No one said anything terrible about the man, not directly, but a number of people felt they had to warn Father Pennant about Lowther's 'lack of discretion.' In other words, Lowther was considered a snoop, a tattletale and a man to be avoided.

As it happened, the person who most insisted on Lowther's bad character was the first to die under Father Pennant's rectorship: Tomasine Humble. Tomasine was no more specific about Lowther's sins than anyone else, but she seemed to take personal offence at Lowther's personality. So, hers were the bitterest condemnations. Mind you, Tomasine had never been known for the good she had to say about others. She was not, herself, fondly remembered, and there were few people at her funeral, when it came. Five, to be exact. Her light, narrow coffin was as simple as could be without being a pine box. It stood in the centre aisle of the church, unencumbered save for, atop the coffin, a framed black-and-white picture of Tomasine Humble as a young woman. Neither beautiful nor homely, the younger Tomasine was merely the beginning of a long distortion whose end was the bent and unhappy old woman Father Pennant had met on his first day as St. Mary's rector.

Tomasine's funeral took place of an afternoon. Light came through the stained-glass portraits of Zenobius and Zeno. The church smelled of the floral perfume one of the mourners wore. Mass was said into the silence of late afternoon in a small town, most of whose inhabitants worked elsewhere. When the service was over, Father Pennant walked from the church with three old women, one of whom matter-of-factly said

— Poor Tomasine. She had a soft spot for priests, you know.

— I thought we were a disappointment to her, said Father Pennant.

— Oh, not at all, said the old woman. Father Fowler was the only man she ever loved. Do you know what 'carrying a torch' means, young man? Well, she carried a torch for that man, poor dear.

–Did Father Fowler know?

– Of course he knew. He loved her too. He joined the priesthood after she married Bill Humble.

– I don't understand, said Father Pennant. Why did she marry Mr. Humble if she loved Father Fowler?

– We'll never know, said the old woman. They were quite strange, those two.

Startled by sunlight as they left the church, the old woman gripped Father Pennant's arm and went carefully down the steps, all thought of Tomasine and Father Fowler gone as she tried to keep herself from falling. Her companions held on to the railings and cautiously stepped down, as if stepping into uncertain waters.

At the end of the day, after Tomasine had been buried, Father Pennant asked Lowther what he knew about Mrs. Humble and Father Fowler.

– Nothing, answered Lowther.

– Did they love each other?

– I really don't think so, Father. In all the years I worked for him, I never heard Father Fowler mention her more than a handful of times.

– Well, Tomasine's friends were convinced ...

– I think Tomasine was convinced too. But she was an odd woman. No offence to the dead. She never had a kind word for Father Fowler.

– You know, I'm not sure she had a kind word for you either.

– Yes, I know. But she's not alone there. Not many people trust me.

– I'm very sorry to hear it.

– No, no. They're right. I haven't always been the best of men.

It wasn't clear to Father Pennant what type of man Lowther wished to be or what type of man Lowther would have called 'good.' Lowther's dislike for his own younger self seemed to be the point. He had been born in Petrolia in 1949, his parents' only child. His father, a bitter and angry man, died when Lowther was twelve. After that, Lowther had become the man of the house, spoiled by a mother who doted on him. By the time he was fourteen, he was, he said, good for nothing. He lied, stole, drank and did things of which he was now deeply ashamed.

He would almost certainly have lost his soul, but that he was intelligent and sensitive despite himself. The cruel things he did began to seem tiresome, mindless and insignificant. So, at twenty, he moved to Sarnia and, for no particular reason save that he saw a help-wanted ad in the *Observer*, found work as a private investigator. His work as an investigator was what earned him his bad reputation. He was good – that is, ruthless – at the work's many stations: skip tracing, process serving, testing the fidelity of husbands and wives. For years, he did very well. He earned all the money he wanted until, one day, he abandoned that road as well. Why? There were, it seemed, a number of reasons. Among them was that Lowther could not be certain he was not adding to the misery of the world. He pitied the men and women who couldn't pay for their cars or who lacked the discipline to be faithful to their spouses. They were, he thought, versions of himself. So, in a moment of contrition, he quit his job and deliberately chose to do the things that, at the time, appealed to him least. He moved to Barrow and began to work for St. Mary's. He taught himself to live on next to nothing, and he gave himself completely to menial work.

The first years of his life in Barrow were almost unbearably tedious. He maintained the church's Volkswagen and cooked for Father Fowler. He did the same things, day in and day out. He forced himself to do them without complaint, though the insignificance of his new life ate away at his self-esteem. He began to think that no man who respected himself would settle for the life he had chosen.

And then the moment came without warning: he learned to surrender. It was early spring, a year before Father Pennant's arrival. Lowther had walked out of town in the direction of the Queen. The sun was up. There was a cold wind. And he was at peace with himself. That's all and that was it: nothing sacred, nothing grand or earth-shattering, nothing that could be shared or passed on. A cold wind. A blue sky. But from that day on, his tasks became fascinating to him. The way one washed or wiped dishes, the way one swept a floor or drove a car: all these duties seemed human and inexpressibly interesting. Less had finally led him to more.

— You learned to live differently, said Father Pennant. You became a good man.

— I learned to live differently, but I'm not a good man, answered Lowther.

— What makes you say that? After everything you've told me, you seem like an exceptionally good man. Not many people change their lives the way you did.

Lowther smiled noncommittally and said

— We can talk about this later, if you're still interested, Father. I really should practise now. Otherwise I won't get my two hours in. Is that all right?

— Yes, said Father Pennant. Of course. Sorry to keep you.

Lowther went up to play the cello.

It was difficult for Father Pennant to understand why Tomasine Humble had been so vicious about the man.

Though it's sad to admit, Tomasine Humble's death was not significant in the way the death of a popular person is significant. Her funeral service was not a memorable occasion, save perhaps for the five old people who attended, for Father Pennant who presided and for the men who dug her grave. Then again, the least death has a weight or sensation to it. A community eddies, if only slightly, to fill a place that had been occupied, and it does so mournfully or happily or with indifference. In very little time, all those who had known her, however well, however vaguely, knew that Tomasine had died and that she had been buried. The circumstances surrounding her death were important to some — especially those her age who felt their own deaths were just around the corner — and insignificant to most. That she was dead was the meaningful thing, along with the fact she had left no heirs, no money, no property.

After Tomasine's burial, the ground in the graveyard was more dense than it had been, with another body — like cold, curdled earth —

to digest. The currents of air that visited Barrow had one less person to circle or caress. And the wind as it blew through town made a sound ever so slightly altered. The ants had one less hazard, the birds one less predator, the worms one more meal. The foxes and coyotes could now go about their business without Tomasine Humble in mind. The fish – carp, bass, minnows and catfish, mostly – would have been very unlikely to feel anything at all, save that, in spring and summer, it had been Tomasine's secret pleasure to put her feet in the Thames from time to time, to feel the cold water run gently over them. No more of that hazard for the fish.

But in the end, Tomasine's death was most significant for a series of events it triggered.

George Bigland, the sheep farmer, was Tomasine's second cousin twice removed. Like most in Barrow, he had always found her a sour and unpleasant person. Still, blood is blood, and he would have attended her funeral had he known when it was. Instead, he found out about his cousin's funeral days after Tomasine was dead and buried. He was indignant. Perhaps because he was already having a bad day, this indignation over a slight stayed with him and, at ten in the morning, he decided he'd do no more work for the day. Instead, he spent hours at the Blackhawk Tavern, luxuriating in resentment, drinking a fermented cider called Bad Apple.

Now, because Bigland did not get home until afternoon, he could not correct a problem created by his son: a gate left open. The sheep, Clun Forest ewes, most of them, though unused to gates being left open, were not impressed. They stood around, nibbling distractedly on the grass in the pen. Four of them, however, drawn by the haunting smell of the woods, the trees, the earth in spring, wandered from the pen, going out in search of grass or clover or other things low to the ground. After a while, three of the escapees, having discovered they were not where they thought they were and missing their sisters, began to bleat. Hours later, these three were returned to the pen by Bigland's son. The fourth, however, went off into the woods.

'Eighteen,' the daring sheep, was a striking ewe: thick whitish coat dark with dirt and redolent of lanolin, black-faced, black ears that pointed straight up and twitched at the slightest sound. Her tail was docked and her lower feet and hooves were black. By the time Eighteen discovered she was alone and that there was not much to eat in the undergrowth, she was lost in the woods. She began to bleat, ears twitching, and wandered farther still until she came to the edge of the woods, which was the side of the road. Then, spooked by a sound in the woods behind her, Eighteen ran to the middle of the road where she was struck and killed by a car. Her body flew up, smacked the car's windshield and was thrown to the side of the road.

As it happened, the car was driven by Jane Richardson. Beside her, Robbie Myers had not put on his seat belt. He flew forward, his head smacking hard against the windshield. He hurt his neck, shoulder and back. He had a concussion and muscle strain, and he was in shock. But there was blood everywhere, so his injuries looked even worse than they were. Without a second thought, Jane, who had not been hurt, drove to the hospital in Barrow.

It's exaggerating very little to say that everyone in Barrow who knew Jane Richardson or Robbie Myers learned of the accident within minutes of it happening. 'Everyone' naturally included Anne Young, who was disheartened by the news, and Elizabeth Denny, who now knew for certain that there was an unclear connection between her fiancé and Jane Richardson.

In this way, Tomasine Humble, Eighteen and Elizabeth Denny were obscurely united across a number of divides.

For Anne Young, the question was how to start a conversation neither she nor her niece wanted to have.

After the accident, the rumours about Jane Richardson's relationship with Robbie became more frank. The worst things were said as if they were true. For instance, that Jane and Robbie had been fondling each other while driving, that Jane had not been looking where she should have been, that Robbie and Jane, with their

motor-car sex, were a bad example for younger kids, that the Richardsons and the Myers were (had always been) bad parents. Didn't
Fletcher Richardson know his daughter was screwing a man with a
fiancée? No one actually *said* 'screwing,' but that's only because the
word was superfluous, it being perfectly obvious that that's exactly
what the two were doing; perhaps even doing it in the car *as* they hit
Bigland's sheep. And didn't Dinah Myers know her son was putting
his money in the wrong bank? What a state we'd reached when
parents couldn't control their children. And what about poor Elizabeth Denny in all this? Wasn't there a kind soul out there to tell her
what was going on between her fiancé and the town floozy? (Well,
Jane Richardson wasn't the town floozy per se. There was competition
for the title. None of the Greenwood girls, the ones who lived off
Tenth Line, could darn a sock or cross a street without fucking.
And Melanie Beauchamp was a known nymphomaniac, having
done her own brother. But still, young Jane was certainly headed in
that direction.) Not that everyone was against Jane. A sizable faction
felt sympathy for her. If Liz Denny couldn't keep her man, why
should that be held against Jane Richardson or even against Robbie
himself? True love is a mysterious thing. And God works in mysterious ways. So, let Liz Denny move on. There was bound to be someone else for her around the corner.

No one related the gossip to Anne Young directly. That would
have been unkind. Even those who disliked her had, at this point,
to be circumspect. But shades of meaning were conveyed in the
secret language of spite: a too kind look, a hypocritical touch on the
arm, a pointed chattiness that was as prickly as the leaf of a thistle.
Anne could feel in others the raw urge to ask if she'd heard about
Jane and Robbie, if she knew about them, if Elizabeth had heard, if
Elizabeth minded, if the wedding was still on.

The wedding. That was the big thing. Anne herself was dying
to ask about it. Rather than avoid the subject, as her husband
advised, or wait until Elizabeth brought the matter up on her own,
Anne decided to ask her niece directly. She waited until one

afternoon when Elizabeth had just come back from work at the bakery. Her niece had made herself a cup of tea and a piece of toast when Anne asked

– Liz? Are you and Robbie still getting married?

They were in the kitchen. The fridge's hum sounded almost aggressive. The afternoon sun was so bright Anne had had to get up and pull the half drapes closed so there was enough shadow to make sitting at the table bearable.

– Yes we're getting married, Elizabeth answered. What makes you think we're not?

– Well, I'm sure you heard about Robbie and Jane Richardson. Their accident?

– Aunt Anne, what does that have to do with anything? He was in the car with Jane and she drove into a sheep. You want me to cancel my wedding for that?

– I don't *want* you to cancel your wedding, sweetheart. I want you to do whatever feels right.

Elizabeth had eaten her toast and gooseberry jam. The crumbs clustered on the white plate looked vaguely like a face: eyes, nose, a small mouth. The knife she had used for the butter and the one for the jam were crossed like an elongated X on the table, until she took them up and put them in the sink.

– You know, Anne continued, there's a lot of talk about Robbie and Jane seeing each other. I don't think anybody knows anything for sure ...

– If nobody knows for sure, why do they all talk about it?

– Barrow isn't the city, Liz. You know as well as I do that people around here can talk about cow dung for hours. Talking about you and Robbie must be a relief, when you think about it.

Despite herself, Elizabeth laughed.

– That's true, she said.

This was just the thing she loved about her aunt: Auntie Anne could always find the thing to make her laugh or bring her around. In this matter, though, Elizabeth didn't want to be brought 'round.

She did not want to talk about Robbie or Jane or marriage until she had worked through her feelings on her own.

– I've heard all the same rumours as you, Elizabeth said.

She'd heard more of them and heard them directly, because even people she hadn't spoken to in years felt it was their duty to let her know what a shit-heel Robbie was. Everything was said in the guise of friendly service. Some even expected gratitude in return.

– Robbie wouldn't do anything to hurt me. If he says there's nothing going on between him and Jane, I believe him.

This was not quite a lie. If he had said such a thing, she would have believed him. But, in fact, the night before, he had said the opposite. Not only had he admitted to his relationship with Jane, but he'd insisted he would not give Jane up, though, inexplicably, he still wanted to marry her, Elizabeth. It should have been a simple matter after that. Any self-respecting woman would have slapped his face and left on the spot. Any self-respecting woman would have refused to see him again. But, to her shame, Elizabeth found it wasn't so simple. She knew one thing (that she should leave him) and felt another (that she should stand by him, whatever he did). This is what she couldn't admit to her aunt, for fear she'd seem ridiculous or weak or irresolute, all of which she felt.

The memory of the previous night returned to Elizabeth as she stood at the kitchen sink. The knives clicked on the white enamel and she remembered that Robbie had not wanted to see her after the accident. He needed to rest, he'd said. He didn't want her to see him as he was: injured, depressed.

– But that's when you should see the people you love, she'd answered.

– Can I have a little time to myself, Liz? Please.

Which was when all doubt vanished. There was something seriously wrong. Still, it was not in her nature to be angry or resentful. She had not complained. She wasn't the type to make a scene or cause pain. That may even be what he held against her, that she could not love him the way he wanted. How unfair, because he made her happy. Effortlessly, it seemed.

In any case, she had said she'd wait for him to call or to meet her at the bakery. And a day after they'd spoken, he had come to the bakery. It had upset her to see him: two black eyes, his neck in a brace, wincing as he walked. It had taken great self-control to keep from crying at the sight of him, to keep from taking him in her arms. Her touch would have caused him pain, he'd said. It was even painful, he'd said, to hold hands, but he had come to show her the state he was in, so she could see he hadn't been lying about his need for rest and solitude. Also, there was something he had to tell her, something important.

– About the accident? she'd asked.

– Yes, he'd answered.

But he would not speak to her then, not in front of the bakery. He had not wanted the whole big-eared town to know their business. So, they had arranged to meet in 'their' clearing in the woods behind her uncle's property.

It was early evening when she got there. The sky, visible above the treetops, was red-orange. The woods were quiet and smelled of pine, of mushrooms and of rotten undergrowth. Robbie came some time after her. She heard him before she saw him. He sounded like a large animal, a deer, say, crashing through the woods. Then, there he was beside her, still wearing the brace that made him look so vulnerable. He was alone. (For some reason, she'd been afraid he would bring Jane.)

He wasted no time on kindness.

– I've got something to tell you, he said. I should have told you sooner. I don't know how to say it, except to say it. So ... I'm in love with Jane Richardson too.

It took a moment for Elizabeth to comprehend.

– What do you mean 'too'? she asked.

– I mean I haven't stopped loving you, Liz, but there's Jane too, now.

– You love us both? That's convenient. Are you screwing us both too?

– Yes, I am. I'm sorry. I should have told you.

Well, what could you say to that? And he had the nerve to look contrite, as if he'd broken a plate and forgotten to mention it. She could think of nothing to say. Instead, she wondered what would happen if she punched his neck. Would he die? Or would the brace save him?

– I know this is the worst thing to tell you before we get married, he said. But I still want to marry you. I still love you, Liz.

– How long have you been seeing her?

– A while. Maybe a year.

– You've been sleeping with the two of us for a year?

– I know, and I'm sorry. It's not like there are rules for this, you know. I tried to do the right thing.

– You proposed to me while you were sleeping with someone else. You *proposed* to me.

– I love you and I want to marry you. This doesn't change how I feel about you.

– Why me? Why do I get to be the wife whose husband is screwing someone else and everyone knows except me? Is that because you love me too?

– I knew you'd be mad. I don't blame you. I really don't understand all this any better than you. But I think we should think this through. You know how I feel about you. I swear I love you more than I've ever loved anyone, but I love Jane too. And I'm asking if you would marry me, despite everything.

Up to that moment, all of her emotions had been in a kind of suspension; no single one presided. Elizabeth was furious, humiliated, amused, unbelieving and stunned that the one man she loved, the one man she thought would protect her from shame, could do this to her. And as happened when there were too many emotions to deal with at once, she shut down. Completely. Door after door closed within her, until she was no more than a surface.

44

– I have to go, she said.

And she'd left him in the woods.

After his words in that place, *their* place, how could she be irresolute? There was no chance the two of them would see each other again. So, why talk about marriage? Yet, when her aunt had asked if the marriage was still on, she'd said yes and she'd said yes because she still had feelings for Robbie, whatever may have happened.

On the other hand, though she still loved Robbie, she wanted to get back at both him and Jane for putting her through this misery. Jane she wanted to hurt outright. But Robbie she wanted to hurt in a way that would leave the door open for him. He would have to work to regain her trust, if he wanted it, if her trust mattered to him. She was not certain she would ever forgive him, but she would give him another chance. How this would happen, how she would deal with Jane, she did not yet know. The first thing to do was to tell Robbie she had thought things through, that she would marry him, if he still wanted her. That would buy her time.

So, again, she had not lied to her aunt. As far as she knew, there would be a wedding.

When she had finished washing her plate and knives and again told her aunt that all was fine, she went up to her bedroom. As she often did these days, she took out the prayer book her parents had left, curious to see if there were a prayer for someone in her position.

There were certainly a number of prayers related to love: a prayer to find love, one to keep love and one to regain lost love. There were prayers for those who had never been in love, who had been abused by love, who had been betrayed by love. There were even more, but Elizabeth chose to read this last one, the one for those who had been betrayed:

> *Lord, free me from the flame of this betrayal.*
> *Let this pain pass and with it the love I feel*
> *For my beloved. Though love is your greatest*

Gift, let me put it by and begin again.
Make me anew in the fire of your true love.
Make me in the balm of your mercy. Teach me
The divine art, forgiveness, that brings peace,
And in peace let me know love again, new forged
From the broken remnants of my ruined Self.
              Amen.

This prayer was not what she needed. The time would come for forgiveness and rebuilding, but not yet. Not until she had settled matters for herself.

During his first months in town (with Lowther's guidance and, most often, his company), Father Pennant took to exploring the fields and woods around Barrow: open fields, abandoned farms, fields lying fallow. All of this walking and looking was done to familiarize himself with the new world: shrews, deer mice, milkweed, monarch butterflies, deer flies, horseflies, blackflies, dragonflies. He noted what he saw, where and when things were seen, and he drew (precisely and beautifully) the flora and fauna of the place. His forays brought him considerable pleasure, as well as instilling the sense that he was getting to know the land at the same time as he got to know the people who lived on it.

In all of this, Lowther was a wonderful companion. He was a naturalist of sorts, infallible when it came to birds and trees. He could, for instance, tell most birds by their song, and it was a pleasure to walk with him, if only because it greatly increased Father Pennant's awareness of the sounds this bright world made. Moreover, April and May provided them with ideal weather: sunshine, light rain from time to time, cool nights, more sunshine. The plants were nourished and thriving and it was exquisite to go out on dew-wet mornings to explore the greening: weeds, flowers, cow manure, sheep shit, the wet spoor of deer, coyotes and, in one field, what looked to be the spoor of a bear, fresh.

One day, when Lowther was unexpectedly called away and could not go with him to the old Stephens place, he warmly insisted Father Pennant explore the abandoned farm on his own. The farmhouse looked to be sturdy, though it smelled of wood that had rotted. The barn was ready to collapse on itself, as if a great hand had pressed down on it and burst its roof. Decades previously, the Stephenses had planted apple trees in a modest, ordered grove: thirty trees in tight rows, five by six. At a distance from the apple trees there were other trees (willows, birches and maples), tall, yellowed grasses, this-tles, buttercups and an unexpected clump of purple lilac bushes that intoxicated with their perfume. A brook, a tributary of the Thames, ran across the property: narrow, four feet across, its waters clear as glass, its banks low and rounded to an overhang in places. In and around the brook: turtles, frogs and small fish that swam like living slivers of birch bark. Beyond the brook, a wide, open field, alive with grasshoppers, crickets and mice.

As it had done when he was beside the Queen, the water held Father Pennant's attention for a time. It ran pure and quick, looking like a strand of clear muscle. And it seemed to Father Pennant as if he could have lifted the brook out of its channel, as he would liga-ments and fascia from an animal he had dissected. What was it about the streams in this part of the world?

Father Pennant stepped across the brook at its narrowest point and began to explore the rest of the field. The land was so alive, it felt as if he could have put a hand down into the tall weeds, without looking, and picked up a living creature. And he was thinking how much he would have liked to hold a deer mouse or a shrew in the palm of his hand when he heard a *click* like the sound of a twig snapping and a cloud of gypsy moths rose from the grasses.

That in itself was strange. Gypsy moths usually ate tree leaves. They were the last thing one would have expected to find in the tall grass. But stranger still, the moths flew up as one and formed, with their wings and bodies, two distinct shapes. First the moths aligned themselves in such a way as to create, from Father Pennant's perspective, an elongated loop:

There could be no mistaking this for a random configuration. Then, as if to confirm that very thought – that they had purposely created a loop – the gypsy moths dispersed then regrouped to form a flawless circle:

They fluttered in formation for some time before falling to the ground.

Father Pennant had never seen nor ever heard of anything like this. He was at first puzzled, unable to quite believe what had happened. He had been surprised by the first pattern the moths made (the loop), but he was, as time passed, frightened by the circle they had formed. He could not help feeling that such a perfect circle had some special meaning, a meaning meant for him alone, but he couldn't for the life of him imagine what it might be. It was as if some being had spoken to him in an extraordinary language and expected him to understand. But, if so, *who* had sent the insects to 'speak' with him?

No, there had to be something wrong with the moths. He looked about the field, but though there had been quite a number of them, Father Pennant could find none on the ground. Here was another puzzling thing: it wasn't possible for so many moths to vanish so quickly. Thinking that deer mice must have eaten them all, he gave up his search for moths after half an hour, disappointed. He drew what he had seen: *Lymantria dispar*, brownish-grey with a brown fringe at the bottom edge of its wings when the wings were closed, its antennae like two delicate, minuscule feathers, its body a narrow, umber cylinder with six thin white stripes that transversed it at almost regular intervals. Perfectly common. They had been gypsy moths, no doubt about it, despite the strangeness of their behaviour.

Or had he been dreaming? He waved his right hand before his eyes. And saw it. He cleared his throat and heard the sound. Aside from the fact that he had just witnessed something unaccountable, he was – or felt he was – as normal as could be: a Catholic priest in Barrow at a time of year – mid-spring – when gypsy moths are about.

As he always did when he was bewildered or thought about God's grandeur and mystery, he kneeled down to pray. He kneeled in the weeds, among the insects and rodents, and prayed for enlightenment. What were his duties, now that he had been given a vision?

There was great comfort in prayer. It was not so much that he felt the presence of God when he prayed, though he did at times feel His presence and that always brought him peace. It was that kneeling – head bowed, fingers interwoven and held on his chest – immediately brought to his mind all the times he had surrendered to the mystery that was the world and to the mystery that was God. Comfort came from the continuity of submission. Kneeling, praying, he was himself at his most open and at his most genuinely human: ignorant, hopeful, humble in the face of the unknown.

The man who had gone to the old Stephens field was, for a time, different from the man who left it. The new Father Pennant was rattled and uncertain. On entering the field, he'd believed he was getting to know the county and its people. Barrow and the land around it had struck him as marvellously new, but not mysterious in any metaphysical sense. The certainty that Barrow and Lambton County were 'normal' was taken from him when he saw moths flying in a circle, a fluttering hoop suspended in mid-air. But this uncertainty wasn't certain either. As the days passed, he grew less sure that he had seen the moths in wilful pattern. The whole episode began to seem incredible and he was relieved he'd chosen to keep details of the day to himself. Lowther would almost certainly have thought him unstable.

He might even have forgotten about the moths, but then, while collecting the mail one day not long after his episode in the Stephenses' field, he found a postcard for Lowther. It was from Cartmel Priory, in England. On the front was the picture of an old church. But on the back, where a signature might have been, was a mark: a one inch by one inch square, with an element that reminded him of the loop the moths had made:

Father Pennant kept the postcard until evening when he and Lowther were at the dining room table. Lowther had, as usual, prepared a lovely meal – white fish, olive bread, lemons, capers, a vinaigrette, a tossed salad. He seemed slightly distracted, or perhaps more thoughtful, but it did not detract from his duties. (The rectory would smell of the olive bread he'd made, for days.)

– Lowther, said Father Pennant, a postcard came for you today. I hope you don't mind, but I was struck by this lovely woodcut on the back, so I hung on to it for a bit. Do you know where the woodcut comes from?

Lowther took the postcard.

– Yes, he answered. This is from Heath, the man who was with me when we first met. He was adopted, but a long time ago he found out his real family's descended from William Caxton, the owner of the first printing press in England. That woodcut is Caxton's symbol.

– Oh. It looked like a rune.

– Nothing that exotic. Just a signature. You know, Heath and I have known each other since grade school. And he's been using that woodcut for a long time. I don't even notice how it looks anymore. It is beautiful, though, isn't it?

– What does he do for a living?

– That's hard to say. He used to be a farmer. Then he worked for Massey Ferguson. Then he made a lot of money selling a fertilizer he invented. He still farms a little, but now, I think, he mostly invents things.

– I'd like to meet him again, said Father Pennant. We never got a chance to talk.

So it was that, three weeks after the incident with the moths and a week after Heath Lambert had returned from the Lake District – where he'd been travelling – Father Pennant was in a house at the outskirts of Oil Springs waiting for Lambert to come in from a back garden where he was gathering rhubarb leaves to use in an insecticide.

Though they were the same age, Heath looked much older than Lowther. His hair was brush-cut, which gave him a military demeanour. He was short, about five foot five, with a belly like a sleeping pup. He smiled at whatever was said or whatever he himself said. It left the impression Heath could give or take any news with equanimity. At least, that was Father Pennant's impression, until he realized that Heath's smile was something of a nervous tic, that an alternate indicator of Lambert's thoughts and feelings were his eyes: dark brown, almost unblinking, serious. It was disconcerting to feel unsure about how to read a man's face, to be unsure if Heath were friendly or slightly hostile. And it was difficult – or difficult for Father Pennant – not to mistrust him.

From the outside, Heath's home appeared to be a solid, old-fashioned red-brick farmhouse with a few solid, red-brick additions here and there. Inside, the house was a bewildering number of connected warrens. This stairway led there and that hallway led somewhere unexpected and on his first tour through the house Father Pennant thought he'd need a map to find any particular room again. As well, every room seemed to be in disarray, with books, papers and magazines scattered about. Some of the rooms were labs of a sort, with cages for white mice or weasels and sand farms for ants, worms and shrews. The whole place was in a kind of organized chaos, and Lambert apologized constantly for the state of his home.

Although Heath Lambert was, clearly, a brilliant man, he was a dull talker. The longer he spoke about something, the more tiresome that thing became. Lambert himself took evident pleasure in explaining things at length. So, when Lowther asked his friend what he had been up to 'in the last while,' Lambert went on for an hour describing the minutiae of his latest endeavours: from trying to discover a natural insect repellent to devising ways to defoliate and kill sick or infected trees.

As Lambert spoke, Father Pennant gradually lost interest in the deadly potential of weeds, herbs and animal by-products. He listened, more and more distractedly, looking out the living room window at a vast, uncut lawn, beyond which were the first houses of Oil Springs. The sky through the living room window was blue behind the cirrus clouds that looked like bloated, white writing. Inside, the air was a little stale, but from time to time a breeze would come through one of the windows, bringing with it the scent of grass and weeds.

Distracted by the sky and the breezes, Father Pennant was caught off-guard when Lowther asked him

– Is that all right?

– Yes, Father Pennant answered instinctively. Yes, of course.

So, when they got up to follow Heath, he had no idea what they were going to see.

They went up to the second floor, walked along a long hallway, then along another, and stopped in front of an orange door.

– Be careful how you step, said Lambert. And please close the door behind you.

Then all three of them entered a room that was, almost literally, filled with gypsy moths. The moths covered the floor, ceiling, walls and windows. There were tables along one wall. On the tables: aquaria.

In the aquaria: leaves and moths. In the centre of the room was a table with a chair, over the back of which was a yellow sweater. On this table were a number of notebooks. On the notebooks: gypsy moths.

Father Pennant was afraid to step anywhere, for fear of crushing the moths. Heath went about in stockinged feet, shuffling rather than walking. He moved his feet on the wooden floor without lifting them, trying to push the moths out of his way.

– Here it is, Lambert said. I've been working with these critters for years.

Stunned (and also somewhat alarmed), Father Pennant said

– I'm sorry. I must have missed something. *What* have you been doing?

– Defoliation, said Lambert. Targeted defoliation. You must have drifted, Father. I'll start from the beginning.

If Heath was at all inconvenienced by this repetition, he did not show it. After brushing the moths off a wooden chair, he invited Father Pennant to sit. Father Pennant sat and, after a few minutes, was covered by moths, some of which he gently brushed from his neck and forehead as Lambert spoke.

Having made much money with his slow-release nitrogen fertilizer, Lambert had gone to the University of Guelph to study biology and psychology, two subjects that had always interested him. His courses in biology led to specialization in entomology. His study of insects led him to wonder if there was any demonstrable insect psychology. He wrote a thesis on 'hive-mind neurosis.' And over the years, he devised a number of experiments with insects, moths in particular. One day, while feeding gypsy moths' larvae, he cut an oak leaf into narrow strips and lay the strips in a pattern. The gypsy larvae naturally followed the pattern their food made. And following many experiments, Lambert found, to his own surprise, that after a time, if the pattern of the leaves was always the same, the moths that emerged from the larvae had a tendency to fly in the pattern their food had made. That is: if, every day for a certain period of time, a larva's food was laid out in a circle, the moth it became would, when it was flying, fly in a circle. With time, he found he could get gypsy moths to fly in circles or triangles or even more elaborate patterns. Of what practical use was this insect husbandry? Lambert thought up any number of uses. For instance, he was almost certain he could train moths to flutter together to make business insignias or business marks. It seemed to Lambert that his moths might even, one day, take the place of skywriting or fireworks. Yes, it was too early to tell if his ideas were workable on a large scale, but he was certain a generation of moths would come along, a generation trained and bright enough to flutter in commercial patterns.

On hearing about Heath Lambert's work, Father Pennant was, to say the least, skeptical. It seemed to him that Lambert was telling tall tales, though the man's constant smile made it difficult to judge how much he believed what he said. It was clear, however, that Heath Lambert, and perhaps Lowther as well, had had something to do with the gypsy moths he'd seen in the Stephenses' field. In the silence that followed Heath's account of moth advertising, Lowther and Lambert stared at him, as if waiting for a reaction. They seemed to expect something from him. In fact, Lowther asked

– Did you want to say something, Father?

But what was he meant to say? He felt relief and sadness. He was relieved that what he had seen in the field was not miraculous. It had not been a sign from God. He did not have to rethink his role on earth. Yet he was also strangely disappointed. For a while, there, in the Stephenses' field, he had recovered his awe before the divine. These men may have been responsible for its recovery, but they were now the cause of its loss.

He considered telling Lambert he'd seen gypsy moths execute patterns in a field near Barrow, but when he thought to say so, he felt a strange reticence. Though neither Lambert nor Lowther had been in the field with him, it was (curiously) as if both knew what he'd been through and were waiting for his testimony. Not wishing to play a game whose rules he did not understand, Father Pennant said only

– I hope your experiments are successful, Heath.

– Why is that, Father?

– Because I can see you love your work.

– That I do, said Lambert. Thank you, Father.

Understandably, Father Pennant lost some of the lightness he'd felt during his first weeks in Barrow. His encounter with the gypsy moths – and Heath Lambert – put him off balance. He was now more acutely aware of himself as an outsider. Still, Barrow had not entirely alienated him. And to commemorate the end of his second month in town, he went to the bakery, looking for a loaf of the bread Harrington himself had sold him on his first day.

Pushing the door to the bakery open, he immediately smelled the kaiser rolls that had recently come from the oven and were now cooling in a wooden bin. He took two rolls and then, seeing the bread he wanted on a shelf, he took two of those as well. To his surprise, the bread too was warm and pliable and smelled of yeast and walnuts.

– Good morning, Father Pennant.

Elizabeth Denny, the bakery's cashier and assistant manager, smiled, took the bread from his hands and put it in two paper bags.

– This is wonderful bread, said Father Pennant.

– Yes, I think so too, said Elizabeth. You're lucky you came when you did, though. There aren't usually any left by now.

Father Pennant thanked her, then stepped out into the sunny mid-afternoon world that smelled of dust and gasoline. He had walked half a block or so when he was stopped by Elizabeth, who tugged lightly on the sleeve of his soutane.

– Father, she said, I'm sorry to bother you. Do you mind if we talk a little?

– I don't mind at all, said Father Pennant. What is it?

– Maybe we could go to Barrow Park, she said. I can sit and eat my lunch there.

– A good idea. I'll even join you. I don't think I can keep my hands off at least one of these kaiser rolls.

They walked together to the centre of town where Barrow Park, a circle of grass some two hundred yards in diameter, stood partially shaded by an imperfect semicircle of willows. In the centre of Barrow Park was a statue of Richmond Barrow looking like an Old Testament prophet. He stood, or his bronze double stood, in formal clothes pointing toward the heavens while staring in the distance at whatever world it is the bronzed see. In the park there were four benches disposed around the statue. Elizabeth and Father Pennant chose the one facing Barrow himself and talked about insignificant things while they ate: a lamb sandwich, in her case; a still warm kaiser roll, in his.

When they had finished eating, they talked about the coming Barrow Day. And then Elizabeth unceremoniously asked

— Father, do you believe it's possible to love two people at the same time?

Father Pennant, taken aback, did not know how the question was meant. He had heard the same rumours as everyone else but he still found the question odd, coming as it did from a woman who was, as far as he knew, soon to be married. This was the second time she'd caught him off-guard with a question about love. She had not called the wedding off, but perhaps she was having doubts about marriage. As gently as possible, he asked

— Are you in love with someone other than Robbie?

Elizabeth laughed: a dry, unconvincing sound.

— No, she said. I've just been thinking about love lately. I think you know why.

— Oh, I see, said Father Pennant. Yes. Well, let me think … I don't have a lot of experience but when I was in love there wasn't room for anyone else in my heart. I can't imagine being equally filled with two true loves at the same time. So, my first answer would be no. I don't think it's possible. What do you think?

— I don't know, answered Elizabeth. I don't see how you can love more than one person at a time. But then God loves us all equally, doesn't He?

– Yes, but the love we feel for each other is different from the love God has for us. Our love is an echo of divine love. That's what I think, anyway. I don't know. It may be possible for a man to love two women or for a woman to love two men, but how would this poor person live?

– Mormons can have more than one wife, can't they?

– Yes, but most of them choose not to. Too difficult. Still, to answer your question: maybe a man can feel equal love for two women, but my advice for that man would be to find the one woman who truly completes him.

The sun had moved to the west, but it was still almost as bright as noon. The park's pigeons had more or less camped out before them, walking back and forth, mindfully unmindful, as if to say 'We're only here taking sun, we want nothing from you,' heads as if pecking at the air, the occasional *rrroo* sounding as one or two of the birds fluttered their wings and rose before setting down again. After a while, the weight of the birds' waiting impressed itself on Father Pennant's imagination. He shredded a piece of his remaining kaiser roll and scattered its morsels in an arc, so all the birds could have a chance at the bread.

– I don't think you're wrong, Father, said Elizabeth. But what if some people are more gifted than others at loving? We can't all run as fast as the fastest. Maybe we can't all love as deeply as the deepest either.

– You *have* been thinking about all this, said Father Pennant. But let me ask you a question. How would you know that a man loved two women equally? How could you tell? Isn't that something only he would know?

The pigeons, joined now by aggressive sparrows, were in a kerfuffle, jostling, flying or trying to fly off with the bigger pieces of bread. Looking at the birds, one had the impression the ground was alive with grey, white and brown feathers, wings and bird heads.

– He'd have to prove it, said Elizabeth. You give him a choice and if he can't choose one woman or the other, he loves them both the same.

– There you go, said Father Pennant. But if he can't choose, he'll be like that donkey who can't choose between two equal piles of hay and dies of starvation. Buridan's ass. That's the donkey's name. You can imagine how amusing that name was when I was in seminary.

Elizabeth smiled politely, though she was not looking at him directly.

– I've got to get back, she said. Thanks for talking to me.

– I enjoy talking with you, said Father Pennant. Any time you like.

The two of them got up as one, shook hands and went off in different directions. Father Pennant, with his paper bags, one now neatly folded inside the other, walked away thinking of his time at the seminary. From the moment he'd given his life to God, joy had come into his soul, and joy was with him still, at times, though he no longer found God at the centre of his happiness. Nature was often there – as if in God's place – and, now he thought of it, it felt at times as if he served two masters or was himself devoted to two loves. Perhaps he'd been hasty in suggesting a man could not love two women equally.

Elizabeth, for her part, was grateful for Father Pennant's advice. She understood him to have said that it was not possible to love two people at once. So, how would she get Robbie to choose between her and the woman whose name now sounded like a nasty word, Jane Richardson?

III

JUNE, JULY AND AFTER

George Bigland had gone to Milwaukee for vacation and he had taken his sons with him. His wife was a capable woman. She had to be, given Farmer Bigland's habits: principally, drink and self-pity. She could have run the farm with her daughters alone, but Bigland had asked Robbie Myers to help out and Robbie had taken time away from work on his father's farm to tend the sheep.

There was nothing new about this arrangement. Robbie had been helping to tend the sheep since he was a boy. Bigland and Robbie's father (also George) had been best friends since childhood. There had even been some hope that Robbie would marry one of the Bigland girls and unite the families. But Robbie had feelings of his own, it seems. He fell in love with Liz Denny, the orphan, and this love had disappointed his father, the Biglands and the Biglands' daughter Anne, who'd had a crush on Robbie from the time when they were young enough to bathe together.

Robbie preferred to tend cows. He was used to cows. He could tell when a cow was sick or healthy or simply wanted milking. With sheep it was all slightly foreign to him. There were always too many of them, gathered together to protect themselves. And it was difficult to care about a clump of bleating creatures whose fleeces were so lanolin-saturated your hand would come out of a fleece greasy and stinking of sheep. He might, eventually, have grown used to the physical fact of sheep, but he could not get used to the irritation of watching over them. Bored while shepherding, he had too much time to think. And having time to think, he had time to make himself unhappy.

These days, time with himself was especially hard to bear. He had told his fiancée, a woman he loved, that he was also in love with another woman. Worse, he was screwing the other woman, though he still hoped to marry his fiancée. There was no getting around how foolish that hope sounded. Looking over the sheep as they jostled and bleated, he could think of nothing but the hurt and resentment in Elizabeth's eyes when they'd spoken. She had not believed he loved her, and he had walked back home upset because he *did* love Elizabeth. That she had not believed he loved her and Jane equally was to be expected. No one believed him. It seemed the world could not or would not believe that his predicament was not, strictly speaking, a sexual matter. His friends imagined him first in the arms of one, then in the arms of the other, a situation they all thought enviable. But how different the reality. He had, in fact, gone directly from one bed to the other, perhaps half a dozen times, but what harrowing times they had been. Jane's pleasure was in having him *before* Elizabeth did. And on occasion, she had tried to exhaust him, letting him up from bed only when she was sure his prick was 'useless.'

A group of sheep had separated from the flock. As much as it was possible for sheep to look suspicious, they looked suspicious. To give himself something to do, he watched as Clyde, the border collie, harassed and nipped the wayward ones back to the group. This distraction lasted only a moment. No sooner were the sheep where they should have been than Robbie was again defending himself against his own opinions and those of the world. What people could not see, he thought, was that Jane and Elizabeth were entirely different. If he had also been in love with someone *like* Liz, well, then, yes, perhaps he could have been considered unfaithful. But where Elizabeth was considerate, careful and gently loving, Jane was unpredictable, selfish and a whirlwind. Where Jane was restless, inventive and adventurous beyond common sense, Elizabeth was constant, patient, adventurous only where the ground was well-known. Jane was physically solid, and he could lose himself in her body. Liz was graceful, her arms and legs like ivy about him. And then there was the matter of company. He could spend hours and hours happily alone with Liz, the two of them walking through the woods or watching old movies. Jane was bored by trees and refused to watch movies that didn't feature naked bodies and high death counts. He could not imagine living with Jane as man and wife, but neither could he imagine a life without Jane there to keep him from drowning at home. So, he loved both equally, knew he could marry Liz, not Jane, and was certain his life would be miserable without both of them in it.

Just as he was beginning to worry about himself in earnest, Robbie's thoughts were, mercifully, interrupted by Anne Bigland. He saw her approach in the distance, bringing him his lunch in a wicker basket. Though they had little to talk about these days, he was relieved at the sight of her. Stepping on birch twigs that clicked and snapped beneath him, Robbie went out to meet her. He was followed at a respectful distance by Clyde, the most mild-mannered border collie there has ever been.

— I hope you're hungry, said Anne. Mom made you three sandwiches, 'cause she wasn't sure what kind you'd want. And there's coffee and orange juice.

— Lunch is the best thing about watching sheep, said Robbie.

— I know, said Anne. Are you bored? I could keep you company.

— I wouldn't mind if you did stay awhile. I'm bored as hell. If it wasn't for the stray dogs around, you could leave these sheep on their own. They're not going anywhere.

Clyde, soul of discretion, lifted his muzzle slightly, allowing himself a circumspect sniff of Robbie's sandwich. He then sat perfectly still: his way of getting attention. And seeing how still Clyde sat, Robbie pulled a morsel from his ham sandwich and offered it to the dog. With the most discreet of motions, a tilt of his head and a flash of pink tongue, Clyde took everything that lay on Robbie's palm. He swallowed the piece of ham sandwich and, once again, sat up straight and stock-still.

– Everything okay these days? Anne asked.
– Yeah, everything's okay.
– You still getting married?
– Looks like it.

The three of them – Clyde, Robbie, Anne – stood or sat quietly. Robbie was grateful for company, but there was nothing he wanted to say to Anne Bigland and, as usual, nothing she could bring herself to say to him, a habit of shyness having set in long before this. Her crush on him was obvious to all. It was clear even to Robbie himself and he was not an observant man.

Not far from them, the sheep began to bleat. A wind troubled the grasses and brought the smell of pine with it. Anne's hair blew in her face and she tucked the strands behind her ears. It occurred to Robbie that she was beautiful. If he'd had a sister, he thought, this is exactly how he would feel for her.

– Do you want some of this sandwich? he asked.

Though she wasn't hungry, she took half the peanut butter and crab-apple jelly sandwich and ate with him.

Jane Richardson loathed Barrow and rural Ontario and anything that smacked of 'flora and fauna.' She was unsettled, and angry at having been born and raised in Barrow, Lambton County, Ontario, Canada. She thought it an injustice that she had not been asked if she wanted to be of this place, this county, this land. It was difficult to know whom to blame for her 'birth in exile,' so she blamed whomever it pleased her to blame: her parents, God, the land or her sheep-like, complacent fellow citizens.

Jane was not born with loathing for southern Ontario. Her first memories of Barrow were good, if banal: a dying bird in her parents' back garden, burrs sticking to her school dress and scratching her thighs when she sat down, snow at Christmas, a strong wind plucking an umbrella from the ground and daintily planting it in a field some distance away. There were thousands of such impressions, and all of them added up to a childhood. As she grew up, however, the bright memories faded or were pushed aside so that, by twelve, she could not have named anything interesting about Barrow. The list of great things it did not have, on the other hand, grew wildly: from the general (Barrow did not have a bar that served elegant drinks) to the specific (Barrow had no Sphinx, no Louvre, no Hagia Sophia). By the age of twelve, Jane Alexandra Richardson was aware that she had been born in a backwater.

For some, hatred of home is mixed with a tincture of self-hatred. But this wasn't so for Jane. She did not think it her fault she'd been born in Barrow. Nor did she exclusively blame her parents, both of whom she loved. Her dislike of Barrow was imperturbable and objective. At fourteen, she had promised herself she would leave the town as soon as she turned sixteen. She would move to the United States, to San Francisco, say, and send for her parents when she had made the beginnings of her fortune. But she had not left at sixteen. She'd been too frightened to leave. Her parents had insisted she finish her education, and her friends had warned her about cities and violence. And she had listened. And in listening to others, she'd betrayed herself. And as far as she was concerned, she continued to betray herself with every moment that passed with her still in Barrow.

Now that she was almost twenty-one, she *had* to leave. Otherwise she would be, like her sisters and her sisters' friends, married and stuck with two or three children by the time she was twenty-five. That thought, the thought of herself lumbered with children and trapped in Barrow, made her life almost unbearable.

To state an obvious point that was not obvious to Robbie: Jane Richardson did not love him the way he loved her. She was relieved that, if things went to plan, Robbie would marry another woman. Though it was conceivable Robbie might consider leaving Barrow, Jane believed he was too much of the place. To her, it seemed he belonged to the town she wanted to leave. As far as Jane was concerned, Elizabeth Denny belonged to Barrow as well. Practically speaking, therefore, Robbie belonged to Elizabeth already, and that suited Jane fine.

Now, at about the moment Robbie was speaking to Anne Bigland and playing shepherd, Jane was in Atkinson's Beauty Parlour getting her hair done. It wasn't something she did often, preferring to stay away from the older women who were Agnes Atkinson's clients. But then, every three months or so, while reading *Vogue* or *New York* magazine, Jane would see a hairstyle she found irresistible. Old Mrs. Atkinson could not always reproduce them exactly, but she always tried and, more, always came fairly close, however odd the style might be. The two of them, the hairdresser in her sixties and the restless young woman, would go carefully over the picture (or pictures taken from different angles, if they were lucky), discussing how best to recreate such-and-such an effect, what to do at the back when there was no picture of the back of the model's head and so on. Then Agnes Atkinson would do her best to copy the style in question.

On this day, the hairstyle Jane found in the pages of *Vogue* was one that made it look as if the model had just stepped out of bed: *au naturel*, as if a hairdresser hadn't touched her.

– What will they think of next? said Mrs. Atkinson.

But it gave her pleasure to do this thing that no one but Jane Richardson would ask her to do. 'Can you do my hair so it looks like you haven't done it?': this idea was, for Agnes Atkinson, very close to a metaphysical proposition. It was right up there with the tree falling in the forest and making – or not making – a sound.

Agnes had washed and shampooed Jane's hair, and she was about to cut it when Elizabeth Denny came into the salon. All talk stopped.

The only sound was the sound of the hair dryers. And, of course, no one knew quite where to look. There were seven women in the salon when Elizabeth entered. Three stared at Elizabeth, then turned to Jane. Three looked at Jane, watching for a reaction, and one woman stared at Elizabeth, shocked that she had committed such an obvious faux pas. After a while, all seven looked elsewhere. Those who had been staring at Jane stared at Elizabeth and vice versa, while the three who had been looking from one to the other carried on looking this way and that.

Without looking at Jane, who was (warily) looking at her, Elizabeth sat in a chair by the door. She picked up a magazine that lay on the low table: *Maclean's*, a pointless rag that she associated with doctors' offices and outhouses near Goderich. Without looking up at the others, Elizabeth turned to the back of the magazine, staring at an article by some frothy blowhard before reading the account of a film about vampires and the review of a novel about a dying child.

The tension that had come at Elizabeth's entrance went (somewhat) underground, lightly torched by the meaningless words that sprang up, like small fires, to distract from this confrontation between a woman and the woman who – everyone knew – was sleeping with her fiancé.

– Are you staying in town for Barrow Day?

– What weather we're having. My back garden's so dry I have to water it three times a day or it'll likely blow away.

– You know, I never have liked boughten salads.

After a while, when it appeared Elizabeth was not looking for trouble, talk turned to more 'serious' things, though everyone kept an eye on the young women. Until finally, upset by Elizabeth's presence, Jane Richardson said

– Liz, are you here to talk to me?

– Not while you're getting your hair done, said Elizabeth.

– I don't have much time afterwards.

– I don't have much to say.

Elizabeth returned to the book review. Jane, unable to move her head freely as Mrs. Atkinson cut her hair, stared at the mirror facing her, wondering if she'd made a mistake with the style she'd chosen. Was it too odd? But then, whenever she had her hair cut, she inevitably had doubts. Once the scissors got going, she would feel an almost irresistible urge to get up from the chair. On this day, however, Liz Denny distracted her somewhat from her doubts.

The other women in the salon were now more alert than ever. Elizabeth had said 'I don't have much to say.' What could that mean? Would she demand Jane leave her fiancé alone? And what if Jane said no? Would things turn, God forbid, physical? These questions, which would be voiced when the young women had gone, were not simple prurience or love of gossip. Most of the women in the salon knew Jane and Elizabeth. A few had known them since they were little girls, so it was strange to see them like this, rivals for a young man they had also known for years. Others, if they did not know them quite so well, knew their relatives or their teachers or their friends. For all intents and purposes, the women in the salon were related to both girls, if not by blood then by whatever the bond is that a place forges among people.

Most of them were on Elizabeth's side. The one who'd been wronged would have had their sympathy anyway. But Jane, with her American hairstyles, was the kind of person who would do better in some big city, while Elizabeth was one of them. In the struggle between the two women, a communal drama was being played out. It wasn't like a sporting event or a boxing match; it was a test of right and wrong, of morality. For all save Mrs. Atkinson – who favoured Jane – a 'victory' for Jane would represent a terrible wrong. It would deepen their (somewhat hidden) mistrust of Jane's 'Sarnia ways' and turn them even more squarely against her.

In some ways, the best outcome would have been a real set-to, a shouting match such as the one there'd been between Rose Cornwell and Nelly Carr when Nelly, the 'older woman,' had seduced Rose's son: a legendary confrontation that everyone still talked about, though it had taken place ten years previously and Nelly, poor woman, had since died of leukemia. It was good to have these things out in the open, good to argue about right and wrong every so often, but it looked as if Elizabeth and Jane were not going to make their dispute public. Jane sat still as her hair was cut, then she sat beneath the pink beehive that was Mrs. Atkinson's best dryer. Elizabeth waited patiently. Then, as Jane paid and thanked Mrs. Atkinson, Elizabeth rose, said goodbye to everyone and waited for Jane outside the salon.

When both women had gone, someone said

— Finally! Nice to get rid of the smell of home wrecker.

— Don't you say anything bad about Jane, said Mrs. Atkinson. I've known that girl since she was a baby. Never hurt a fly.

Elizabeth and Jane walked for a block or so, awkward in each other's presence, before Elizabeth said

— It's no use being subtle about all this. We both know what's going on. I want to know why you're sleeping with my fiancé.

— I'm not sleeping with your fiancé. He's sleeping with me.

They passed Barrow Park. The statue of Richmond Barrow was pointing to the sky: a light, washed-out blue, the clouds elongated wisps, the wind a persistent breeze that brought a whiff of gasoline, of freshly cut grass and of the dirt that lightly flayed the streets and buildings. Though waves of hatred hit her, Elizabeth kept her temper. Jane lit a cigarette.

— Whether you're sleeping with him or he's sleeping with you, it's the same thing, said Elizabeth. You knew we were engaged.

— I *thought* you were engaged, but engaged men don't usually sleep with anyone except their fiancées, do they? So how was I to know what was going on between you two?

The sound of Jane's voice made her so upset, Elizabeth stopped walking. To cover her emotion, she asked for a cigarette, though she did not smoke, and she was further annoyed when Jane gave her one and then put a hand on hers — to keep it from shaking — as she lit it. Elizabeth drew in the smoke without inhaling. As for Jane:

this was now an interesting game, sophisticated even. Here she was talking calmly to Robbie's fiancée. She allowed herself to wonder what Robbie saw in Elizabeth and then wondered, fleetingly, what it would be like to sleep with Elizabeth, what it would be like for *her* to sleep with Elizabeth.

– I don't want to keep walking away from work, said Jane. If you have something to say to me, say it now.

– You know what I want. I want you to leave Robbie alone.

– Why? Why should I stop seeing him? He loves me as much as he loves you.

– No, said Elizabeth, he doesn't.

– It's no use arguing. He would've left me if he didn't.

After considering this, Elizabeth said

– Fine. Then you should help me make him choose.

– What, choose me or you? I don't see why. I don't mind if he marries you. I think things are going well the way they are. What's the problem, except everybody in this stupid town expects it to be one man, one woman?

– I don't want it to go on like this, said Elizabeth. I want my husband to be with me, not some woman he's addicted to. I'd leave him but I don't believe he loves you as much as he loves me. You're just a phase. But he should make a choice now. That's why I'm talking to you at all. I think if you can get Robbie to do something he wouldn't do for me, it'll prove he loves you more. And that'll be enough for me.

How interesting, thought Jane. Their conversation had gone from something unpleasant and vaguely threatening to something that intrigued her: a wager of some sort. Whatever she felt for Robbie, she was certain of his loyalty and she was even more certain she could convince him to do anything short of poisoning his father's cows. Of course, the prize, if you could call a man a prize, was Robbie, and she was not certain she wanted Robbie for herself. Perhaps, and the thought crossed her mind as she looked at Elizabeth, she would not find Robbie attractive without Elizabeth there to be his wife. Really, what was there in him, when you thought about all this objectively? What was there that one would want to have exclusively? And yet, the proposition was appealing. Jane said

— And I get to choose what to make him do?

— No, answered Elizabeth. I get to choose the thing. It wouldn't be fair otherwise.

— All right. Have you decided what it is?

— Yes. I want him to walk naked into Atkinson's Beauty Parlour and ask Agnes for a haircut.

Elizabeth had thought this through. She knew how shy Robbie was, how much he disliked people seeing his feet, which, she had to admit, were not his best feature. Also, he had a red birthmark beneath his left nipple, like a paint-wet hand had slapped him, then dragged itself around to his back. He did not even like *her* to touch it. So, it was difficult to believe anyone could get him to walk about naked. On the other hand, if Jane did convince him to go into Atkinson's without his clothes, the moment would be a lasting humiliation for Robbie, a humiliation very like the humiliation he had put her through. So, either way, she could not really lose.

— Is that all? asked Jane. I wonder if you know Robbie as well as you think you do. I feel like this is too easy. Is there something *really* difficult you'd like me to get him to do?

Jane Richardson's confidence — or was it insolence? — was unexpected. If she knew Robbie as deeply as she claimed, she should have understood how difficult it was going to be to convince Robbie to go around naked. Elizabeth could not begin to imagine Robbie unclothed in Atkinson's.

— I don't have anything else in mind, she said.

But then, slightly unnerved, she added

— He can't do Atkinson's on Barrow Day, you know. That wouldn't be fair.

— No, getting him to go naked on Barrow Day wouldn't be hard. But, anyway, Atkinson's is closed on Barrow Day. So ...

Jane looked at her watch.

— I've got to go, she said. But it's a deal.

They had got as far as St. Mary's church. The afternoon sunlight touched the windows devoted to Zenobius and Zeno. Jane turned away and walked off. Elizabeth stood by herself awhile, looking up at the illuminated blue lake beside which St. Zeno stood. She reminded herself that she had thought things through. She did know Robbie, knew him better than Jane did. (She wondered if Robbie and Jane did the same things she did with Robbie or was Jane 'better at it' than she was? The picture of Jane and Robbie in bed together — an image she could not ward off — almost made her sick, it was so upsetting.) Yes, anyone betting on who should know Robbie best would, almost certainly, put their money on her, on Elizabeth. And yet, Jane's confidence was disconcerting. So much so that Elizabeth began to regret what she'd set in motion.

As she returned to the bakery, Elizabeth considered how far from herself she had been dragged. Though she'd always been thoughtful, she had never been manipulative or underhanded. Jane Richardson had called manipulation and connivance out of her. In fact, Jane, a different kind of woman, was perhaps more gifted at deceiving, more used to deception. In which case, Jane could get Robbie to do whatever she wanted him to do. But then again, no, she had thought things through. Even if it were possible to convince Robbie to expose himself to the women in Atkinson's, the exposure would humiliate him and, humiliated, he would hold the incident against Jane. All of this seemed to her to be true and irrefutable. Life was unpredictable, yes, but Robbie was not, and she knew him well. She would not have agreed to marry him otherwise, would she?

The afternoon was bright. She heard birdsong. The town of Barrow, which she knew as well as she knew her lover's body, was vivid in the sunlight, like a bauble of itself.

Though they had arranged to see Petersen's gravel pit together, some-where near the last minute Lowther apologized for having forgotten a prior engagement — that is, a lunch with Heath he'd neglected to write in his calendar. He'd left Father Pennant to explore Petersen's on his own, dropping him off some way from the pit so he could enjoy the afternoon sunlight. That is why, at around the time Barrow was vivid for Elizabeth Denny, Lowther and Heath were at Heath's kitchen table talking about the distant past. In particular, they were talking of Lowther's father, a man who'd left his son little save fleeting memories and a defaced book of prayers.

The prayer book was leather-bound. Its endpapers were red and marbled. But the most obvious feature of the book, now, was that all of its two hundred prayers had been blacked out, save one. Old Mr. Williams – that is, Lowther's father – had been eccentric, and the prayer book, which Heath held in his hand, reminded Heath of the old man himself. Though fervently religious, Mr. Williams had reduced the majority of the prayer book's pages to black lines, beneath which one could still read the occasional 'Amen' or 'Lord.' The only prayer left untouched was the final one, a prayer to be said by those whose suffering was unendurable:

> Lord grant me death and let me know
> At last the last of Earth.
> Time has done its work, now let it rest.
> Come darkness and night,
> Set this poor shadow free.

Heath said

– He was a strange man, your father.

– I know, said Lowther, but I've begun to understand him lately.

– You Williamses think too much.

– Yes, but these days it's different. These days I accept that I'm an ignorant man, whatever I learn or take in. And I think that's what my father was trying to tell me when he gave me his prayer book. Out of all these prayers there's only one essential prayer.

– But it's a prayer for death.

– I'm not sure that's the important point. Dad spent his life reading philosophy and, in the end, there's only one prayer he passed on. A handful of words. His way of saying life doesn't amount to much.

— Do you want more coffee? I'm going to have a cup.

Heath took down a white cup and blew in it to remove what looked like an insect leg.

— Listen, he said. Do you know how long it took me to clear those moths out of that room? I'm still finding bits of them.

— Thank you for that, said Lowther. I'm really grateful.

— Did you get what you were looking for?

— I'm not sure what I was looking for, said Lowther.

— Well, what do you think of him now?

— He's young, but I trust him.

— You do? Strange he didn't actually tell us he saw the moths. Your young priest keeps secrets.

— Maybe, or maybe he's discreet. The first thing most people would have done is tell the world about the miracle they'd witnessed.

— True. If I saw a bunch of gypsy moths doing strange things, I'd assume the rest of the world *should* know about it. I mean, why not? You've got to let people know their pests are going loco, you know? I spent hours creating that illusion, but that story about insect psychology was almost as hard. Nearly made myself sick trying to keep a straight face. I should hope you got something out of it. Anyway, what are you going to do now?

— I don't know. But my time's coming. I can feel it. I've got to make myself ready. That's what all this is about, remember? I want to know the man who's going to be travelling along that last road with me.

— I still think you're being pessimistic.

— Heath, my father died at sixty-three, as did his father, as did his father before him. Ten generations of Williams men have died within weeks of turning sixty-three. I've had a good life. I'm not unhappy and I haven't left anyone behind me to die like this.

— I know all that, said Heath. But maybe death isn't as predictable as you think.

— Every year winter comes and every year we're shocked when it snows and people forget to put on their snow tires and someone falls through the ice. No one knows the exact hour of winter, but it always comes somewhere round the same time.

– Hmm, said Heath.

They had been having this same argument for years. Lowther was convinced he could feel death's approach, while Heath was dubious anything clear could be known where death was concerned. Each had been influenced by the other's position, but only a little. There was now in Lowther's mind a small doubt, a niggling sense that, after all, humans cannot know about these things. So, how could he be certain when his end would come? Meanwhile, over time, Heath had begun almost to accept that Lowther knew what he was talking about. He had begun to accept that the collection of atoms called Lowther Williams would dissipate and decay in Lowther's sixty-fourth year. In fact, it was for this reason Heath hadn't minded deceiving Father Pennant. Though the holographic moths and their trip switches had cost him a fortune, it had been something for the two friends to do together, something very like the pranks they had pulled when they were twelve but with a higher purpose: Lowther, convinced he would die soon, wanted to know – to truly know – the man who would administer his last rites, who would pray over him, who would shepherd him into the next world. Heath didn't understand why this was important. He himself didn't care who or what was around when his own spirit left its casing. He didn't believe in a 'next world.' But it mattered to Lowther – his closest friend – and so it mattered to him.

The day outside Heath's kitchen window hemmed and hawed: a lawn mower here, a passing car there, barely a moment's silence. There were wispy clouds and the air was warm. For a moment, the outside smelled of toast and honey, while inside there was the odour of bleach and coffee.

Lowther too was thinking of the days spent with Heath when they were boys, of the things they had done as children. Hard to believe Heath's mother had ever forgiven them for the time when they'd caused her hair to fall out. But she had forgiven them and had spoken of it with amusement until her dying day. But that is the kind of woman Mrs. Lambert was. She could no more have held such a thing against them than they could have done anything but regret it afterwards. And that is what he wanted to know about Father Pennant: what *kind* of man was he? The incident with the moths had been a success. It had brought something out of Father Pennant: his discretion and tact. Good qualities, both. But Lowther wanted to know a little more. He wanted to catch a glimpse of something more deeply hidden. He wanted to know the far corners of Father Pennant's being because, in the end, he needed to know that Father Pennant was the right shepherd for him.

In Lowther's imagining, his own death – for which he was wholly prepared – took place in a room with an accommodating bed, a sun-brightened window, the sky blue, the last voice heard that of a good man who appreciated the accomplishment of death. As he listened to the clinkety-clink the cup made as Heath put it down on a saucer, Lowther tried to imagine Father Pennant at Petersen's gravel pit. Would Father Pennant catch Mayor Fox at the right time? And what would the priest make of it if he did? Lowther remembered the first time he had seen Fox walk on water. It had been disconcerting, a little frightening even. If it was the same for Father Pennant, why then, he – that is, Lowther – had his man.

The gravel pit just outside Barrow was a jewel or a danger, depending. The pit itself was hidden from view behind a bank of trees and some way along a sandy road. It was nearly circular and some sixty feet in diameter. It had been a long time since there'd been any digging and the water in the pit was deep. In fact, its depths had been exactly sounded: thirty feet and seven inches deep at its deepest point and every once in a while a young man or young woman, drunk or disoriented, fell into the water and drowned.

Lowther had left him about a mile from the pit, but Father Pennant happily walked there on his own. He walked by the side of the road, trampling on young thistles, dandelions, chicory and tall grasses. The smell of the weeds clung to his walking shoes and rose up so that, although he was by the side of a highway, it smelled as if he were in an endless field. The laneway that led to the pit was not hidden exactly, but there were no obvious signs that this particular path led somewhere interesting rather than to one of the many hidden properties, abandoned farms or private houses with their snarling dogs. The only hint of the pit's existence was near the locked metal gate before the trees. There, on the ground, was a rotted but still legible wooden sign that read *Petersen's Gravel.*

Feeling slightly foolish and vulnerable, Father Pennant climbed over the fence, as Lowther had advised him to do, and walked the sandy road to the pit. The trees were tall and they partially blocked out the sun, so there was a darkened hush until he came to the clearing. Then: the return of day. The sun shone on a landscape that had been sheared of trees. Before him were hills of reddish sand around which the path snaked. He had rounded a second hill and could see a part of the pit when Father Pennant realized he was not alone. He heard a voice and then, when he rounded another hill, he saw a man, back facing him, standing beside the water.

The man was almost fully dressed: light-coloured suit jacket, matching pants. But he held his shoes and socks in his hands. Not wishing to disturb the man or frighten him, Father Pennant waited quietly at a polite distance, intending to let him finish what sounded like prayers. But the prayers, which began to sound like a strange song, continued for a while. Then, suddenly, the man stepped into the pit and began to walk on water. Having witnessed the 'miracle' of the moths, Father Pennant did not believe what he was seeing. He looked around for something that might explain the lightness of the man or the sturdiness of the water.

There was no one about. The man continued across the water, singing or reciting as he went. The water was rigged, surely. There was almost certainly some solid path just beneath its surface. And smiling at what he imagined to be a wonderful illusion, Father Pennant stepped into the water at or near the very point the man had stepped. It was deep water, though, and he sank. His clothes and shoes weighed him down immediately. Sputtering and panic-struck, he managed to turn himself around and pull himself out of the pit. The water was cold, but he kicked off his shoes, grappled to safety and emerged mud-streaked, soaked and freezing. Turning back to the pit, he was stunned to see that the man was on the opposite side looking at him or seeming to look at him with derision. Poised a moment on the other side, still speaking to himself or to Father Pennant, the man now began his return across the water. If when he had thought it a trick Father Pennant found this water walk charming, he was now frankly frightened by it.

As the man approached, Father Pennant recognized George Fox, the mayor of Barrow. Mr. Fox was not speaking English, nor was he paying the least attention to Father Pennant. He looked only before him, enraptured, speaking in tongues:

– *Mose hsaou ne eeaui aoe meu ne loox an matu uie matu og easui ...*

Hearing these sounds and believing that Fox was possessed, Father Pennant fell to his knees and began to pray. He was in the presence of the diabolical. He knew it. He closed his eyes and said his prayers as loudly as he dared. He was not a timorous man, far from it, but he was terrified to be in the presence of Satan.

He felt a hand on his shoulder and the touch was like fire, despite his wet clothes.

– Father Pennant? Are you all right?

Opening his eyes, Father Pennant saw George Fox looking down at him. Fox had a broad face in which his small, brown eyes were set. His forehead was speckled by freckles. He was mostly bald and his breath was abominable, like sour milk and rotting chicken skin. Above Fox, the sun ignited a small cloud.

– Get thee behind me, Satan, said Father Pennant. I cannot be tempted.

Mr. Fox stood up straight, immediately defensive.

– That's pretty unfair, he said. I'm a politician, so maybe you've heard people say some bad things about me. But I'm as God-fearing

76

as the next man. I may not be Catholic, but that doesn't give you the right to insult me.

Mayor Fox walked away with all the outrage he could muster – very little, as it happened, because he was a generous and warm-hearted man. Not that Father Pennant noticed the mayor's attempt at outrage. He was too busy praying, reciting the psalm he loved best (*As the hart panteth after the water brooks, so panteth my soul after thee, O Lord ...*) over and over, until he felt calm enough to stand. Only then did he look up and take stock of the situation. He was alone, shoeless, wet, his clothes covered with grit. It seemed to him that he had seen the devil disguised as Mayor Fox. And Satan, unlike the gypsy moths, *was* a mystery, as miraculous as loaves and fishes, water and wine. Father Pennant had encountered the Lord of the Flies, and his faith, which had wavered of late, was fully restored.

He shivered as he walked the miles back to town, his feet punished by the stones at the side of the road.

That evening Father Pennant was still too upset to do his duties, too shaken to prepare a sermon for the next day or to visit the old people at Maud Chapman's Home for the Aged. He sat at the dining table, as if turned to lead. Lowther had prepared a lamb roast with roasted potatoes and sweet corn. For dessert he had made a sticky toffee pudding. The pudding had sat out, aromatically blooming in the rectory as soon as it was taken from the oven. Father Pennant, who loved sticky toffee pudding, put his spoon in the pudding, tasted a morsel and dispassionately said

– Thank you, Lowther. It's good.

before putting his spoon down and looking away.

Lowther was, of course, interested in the priest's behaviour, but he sat in silence until Father Pennant said

– Do you believe in evil, Lowther?

– I believe men do unspeakable things, Father. I don't know about evil.

– Evil is the other side of the sacred, said Father Pennant. If there's no evil, there can't be anything sacred either. I know that. I know it is God's will that evil exist, but I wish it were different.

– I can see you're upset, said Lowther. Do you mind my asking what's wrong?

– No, I don't mind, said Father Pennant.

He told Lowther what he had lived through that day: the climb over Petersen's gate, his first vision of Mayor Fox, Fox's diabolical traverse of the gravel pit, walking on water and speaking in tongues, and his – that is Father Pennant's – near drowning and long walk home. When he had heard Father Pennant's story, Lowther said

– I'm sorry I didn't go with you, Father. I understand how you could interpret things as you did. And I can see how much you respect and fear Satan, but there wasn't anything satanic about what you saw. Nothing miraculous either. Mayor Fox should have told you himself, when he saw you so upset. He wasn't walking on water. If anything, he was walking on plastic. I know it'll sound strange to an outsider, but Mayor Fox crosses the gravel pit every year. Several times a year, actually.

There was a perfectly logical explanation for what Father Pennant had seen. What he'd seen was a foretaste of Barrow Day. There were, deeply planted in the gravel pit's floor, tall columns of thick, clear plastic, columns some thirty feet tall, almost entirely invisible to the eye. There were sixty of them. They were beneath the surface for most of the year, but in late summer, the water level fell and you could see them clearly. The tops of the columns were flat and oval, wide enough to accommodate even a large human. The columns were arranged so that a man or woman of average height could walk across the pit with ease. Naturally, when the water was high, as it usually was, you couldn't see the columns and so it looked as if someone were walking on water, though they were actually stepping on the flat tops of the columns. More than that: the words Mayor Fox recited were not an incantation. He hadn't been speaking in tongues. The words, gibberish really, had been written to help whoever was walking across the water know when to step. The pillars were not evenly spaced, so if you walked at the right pace and said the words with the right rhythm, at every third word you could step down with confidence. The timing was important. The words and their rhythm varied according to the height of the person crossing the water. That was all there was to tell, in essence.

No, there was more. This walk across the columns was a relatively new aspect of Barrow Day. The columns had been fashioned and then (with great difficulty) planted in the gravel pit by an artist. The artist, a Russian émigré named Anton Mandelshtam, had meant his 'installation' to represent the freedom one has in a capitalist society. For instance, the freedom to walk across a gravel pit without getting one's feet dirty, to walk above the land as if exalted. No one in Barrow understood the ideas behind Mandelshtam's *Freedom*, but watching a man walk across the pit on glass pillars was, in and of itself, entertaining. The installation was such a popular work that it was absorbed into Barrow Day's festivities, and by the late eighties, the crossing of Petersen's gravel pit came to mark the end of Barrow Day.

— I've done it myself, said Lowther. It's difficult. The tops of the columns are sometimes slippery. You have to pay attention. When he was crossing the gravel pit, Mayor Fox wouldn't really have seen or heard you.

Father Pennant did not know what to say. He believed what Lowther told him and he felt he should have been comforted to learn that what he'd taken for diabolical was, in fact, a kind of civic duty. And yet, he was not comforted.

— You know, said Lowther, it's easy to mistake what we see for things we haven't seen.

Lowther felt contrite for a trauma that was, after all, of his own making. He had meant for Father Pennant to see Mayor Fox cross the gravel pit. He had even hoped Father Pennant would be as stunned as he had been when he first saw the 'miracle.' So, in effect, the timing had worked out perfectly, where Lowther was concerned. On the other hand, Lowther had lived in Barrow for so long he found it difficult to think of the mayor's walk on water as anything that could permanently affect a man. Though he regretted the extent of Father

Pennant's shock, Lowther had learned something important about the priest: Father Pennant was superstitious in just the way Lowther admired. The man believed as fervently in darkness as Lowther himself did. There was now, as far as Lowther was concerned, an unshakeable bond between himself and Christopher Pennant. No more 'miracles' were needed, no more crises for the young priest to deal with. When Lowther's time came, he would be honoured to confess his sins to this man and to leave the world with grace.

But the effect on Father Pennant of this contact with a counterfeit 'evil' was indelible, and it changed him. He was no longer the man Lowther imagined him to be.

After his encounter with Mayor Fox, Father Pennant was wary of Barrow Day. He was not as inclined to join the celebration as he was to observe it.

Every year, harsher penalties were instituted, in an effort to limit the worst offences: public drunkenness, public nudity, public fornication. And every year, these things (drunkenness, nudity, etc.) happened just often enough to bring on both Christian regret and a pagan longing for the next year's celebrations.

Barrow Day began at eleven o'clock with memorial masses said in churches across town. At mass, the townspeople remembered those who had died during the previous year as well as Richmond Barrow himself, long dead but still illustrious. After mass, it was traditional, whatever the denomination, to eat a slice of Barrow bread: a sweet bread (or cake) made with flour, eggs, sugar, coconut, raisins and vanilla. The centre of Barrow bread was where the coconut and raisins (dyed red) were baked in the form of an X above which there was a circle. That is, when one cut a slice of the loaf, it was meant to look as if a red skull and crossbones were in the slice's centre. Though this required some skill to do well, virtually every woman in Barrow could make Barrow bread and make it very well indeed.

At one o'clock, the parade would begin. There were no more than two miles from one end of town to the other, but the parade usually went on two or even three hours, because half of the population was in the procession. Not that the spectators minded the time it took their family and friends to walk from one end of town to the next. It was during the parade that drinking began in earnest. Officially, drinking was not permitted on the streets, but the men and women watching the parade would all drink (much or little) a concoction of soda, rum and dandelion wine: Barrow brew. A little Barrow brew went a long way. Father Pennant – who politely accepted a mouthful from a pigskin – found it unbearably sweet. But it lifted the spirits of most who drank it, so that the parade was the heart and soul of the day.

The parade was not entirely about drink and good cheer. It was also fitfully, strangely beautiful. This was largely due to the handmade and sometimes breathtaking costumes worn by that half of the town that was on display. The parade was also a competition, with 'best costume' elected by a panel of judges. And here, the unusual was prized above all. One year, for instance, first prize was given to Rowland Briggs, a house painter, whose costume made him look like a burning schoolhouse, complete with students and teachers jumping from the upper floors. A year later, the prize was won by John Walker, a garage mechanic, whose costume included an effigy of a school principal hanging from a gallows while flames rose up behind him. Walker's outfit was considered a witty rejoinder to Briggs's costume.

After the parade, there was a breather, a few hours during which people could prepare for the banquet and dance that took place in the old fire hall. And finally, at the end of the night, usually around eleven o'clock, almost everyone – adults and such children who were not asleep or a hazard to themselves – ended up at Petersen's gravel pit where the mayor would walk across the water and so mark the end of the day's festivities.

Father Pennant's first Barrow Day passed like a convulsive dream. It began early with Lowther practicing 'The Song of the Birds,' a mournful piece that cast a spell on the day: quiet, as the sun rose in the faded blue sky, no clouds, the morning smelling of a warm rhubarb compote Lowther served at breakfast.

At eleven o'clock, the church was filled to capacity, most of the celebrants his own parishioners. He smiled at Robbie Myers and Elizabeth Denny – who, conspicuously, sat side by side – and nodded at George Rubie and George Bigland. For some reason, the brooch worn by Ellin Machell, the librarian, caught his attention: praying hands carved in a light blue stone.

After mass, there were more faces and mingled voices.

– How're you, Father Pennant?

– Happy Barrow's Day, Father.

– Father, have you met my cousin Don?

Then they were all eating Barrow bread, a macabre kind of treat, it seemed to Father Pennant, but delicious: the taste of coconut against the sweet raisins. In the end, he sampled the Barrow bread of seven or eight women before returning to the rectory, where Lowther had prepared roast chicken, dill dumplings and, of course, Barrow bread. Lowther's bread was wonderful, but it was also a slight variant: in the centre of his slices there were no skulls and crossbones but only a simple, puffy red circle.

Father Pennant had been invited to be part of the parade but, wary as he was, he chose to watch the procession from the sidewalk. Men and women he had seen here and there passed by on trucks, on tractors, on the back seats of convertibles. It seemed as if every institution in town had put one of its own on the back of something that moved: Lions Club, Rotary Club, 4-H Club, library, fire station, police station. People he had seen behind counters or out in the street waved, smiled and waved, accompanied by recorded music or followed by men playing bagpipes, which, as ever, sounded like small children being tortured into melody.

Most of the costumes were plain. There were *coureurs de bois*, frontier ladies, a handful of Laura Secords and a dozen (faux) Native Canadians. But there were also a number of perplexing or curious disguises. Two in particular struck Father Pennant as remarkable.

The first made its wearer look as if he or she were a large bear. Out of the bear's mouth a bald eagle sprang up with a salmon in its beak. The salmon flipped and flopped as if it were alive and, at intervals, spat hard candy into the crowd. The second costume, more grotesque, was worn by a man on stilts. He looked like a gigantic and unpleasant beetle. The man's white face protruded from the insect's dark mandible. From the lower parts of the insect, balls of foil-wrapped chocolate dropped. The chocolate was perhaps meant to roll to the children watching the parade, but it was inevitably squashed by the people or vehicles that followed, the warm chocolate oozing or spurting from the foil.

Father Pennant stood in one spot all parade long. So, he was not aware of any incidents that took place in other parts of town. He heard about some of them in the bits of conversation he caught from those who passed by. For instance, he heard about two or three drunks, the most unruly of whom seemed to be George Bigland.

– Only thing he ever does is drink and fuck sheep, said someone.

– Yeah, it's a vicious circle, answered someone else.

Also, Esther Greenwood, whom Father Pennant knew as soft-spoken and modest, had exposed her breasts, as she had been doing for years in an effort to bring attention to the various cancers that afflicted women in Barrow. When Esther had first decided to bare her breasts, some fifteen years previously, she had indeed brought attention to herself and her cause. But times had changed. Few people paid attention to her, and the police, one of whom inevitably brought a sweater to the parade, covered Ms. Greenwood up as soon as she disrobed. Over the years, other women had bared their breasts in sorority with Esther, but not this year.

Two hours after the parade had begun it ended. People dispersed. Those who were incapacitated were helped away. And for a moment Father Pennant saw the town cleared (or at least clearing) of people. Plastic cups and paper plates moved like little animals across the streets and lawns in the centre of town. As he was walking back to the rectory, the street cleaners came. A small battalion of men with push brooms began to restore order. It struck Father Pennant as an oddly sinister sight.

Just as sinister was the lone man astride the shoulders of Richmond Barrow's statue. The man seemed to be drunk and, from time to time, called out for what Father Pennant assumed were his friends. That is, he shouted 'George' or 'Johnny' or 'Arlene.' There was no one around him. He had been abandoned. Nor, as far as Father Pennant could tell, did the man want to come down. As the priest passed, the man stopped shouting and was polite.

– How are you, Father? Having a good day? I wish there were more apples, don't you?

And then, as if he'd recalled something crucial, he began shouting out his names again.

– Arlene! Johnny! George!

It was as if a moment of sanity had passed through a madman, like a shiver animating someone feverish.

Father Pennant did not go to the dinner and dance at the firehall. Lowther had warned him that, the previous year, thirty people had been sent to the hospital by coquilles St.-Jacques that had proved to be a ruthless laxative. Father Pennant and Lowther ate at the rectory.

At eleven, they took up their candles and flashlights and walked to the Petersen gravel pit, met on the way by dozens of festive others. For Father Pennant, this walk in darkness, flashlights guiding their steps, was the most striking part of the day. Yes, some of those who walked were so drunk they had to be helped, but most were buoyed by a spirit that came from somewhere beyond the nameable. It was a kind of pleasing fright, this being out under the star-filled sky, the darkness and mystery only slightly lessened by company.

The gate to the gravel pit had been opened. The sound of laughter and a chaos of light accompanied Father Pennant and Lowther through the trees, around the hills and to the pit. And here there was a marvellous vision: hundreds of people gathered around the water, encircling the gravel pit. And it seemed each of the hundreds held his or her own lighted candle. The candles were tall, short, thin, thick. Some were scented; most were not. So many candles that the night was lit up by flickering flames. The black water in the pit was flecked with candlelight, the whole surface looking like a plane of anthracite on whose edges hundreds of fireflies had settled. It was one of the most beautiful things Father Pennant had ever seen.

Then, just before midnight, there was a commotion as Mayor Fox made his way to the edge of the pit. The townspeople began to sing, quietly at first but then with confidence. They sang a hymn whose melody Father Pennant did not recognize but whose words he knew well.

– The Lord is my shepherd; I shall not want ...

When the hymn was finished, Mayor Fox, speaking through a bullhorn, thanked everyone for coming. He spoke about how bountiful the preceding year had been. He promised the coming year would be just as good. He said the names of those who'd died during the previous year. Then, asking for quiet, he put aside his bullhorn and began to speak his necessary gibberish.

– Uine iat eooe iut xosl oox naz iu setu ...

The crowd was now so quiet one could hear the flippety-flip of candle flames bending and rising in the wind. Mayor Fox stepped off the shore and into the black water. Most momentarily held their breath. The only sound, save for the wind and candle flames and the splash of water, was the voice of Mayor Fox reciting his nonsense as he walked in broken rhythm across the top of the gravel pit. Only when he had made it from one side to the other was there a collective sigh and then a great cheer. Mayor Fox had succeeded and his success was theirs. Joy spread through the crowd in waves, like a communal, prickly blush. And for a moment, there was harmony. And then, one by one at first, the crowd extinguished its candles. Flashlights were turned on and slowly the people of Barrow walked back to town together.

Despite himself, Father Pennant was unnerved by Mayor Fox's walk across the pit. As he went home, the day returned to him in all its uncanny aspects: from the sweet red skulls to the fireflies on anthracite, from the face in the insect to the drunk on Richmond Barrow's back. It occurred to him that Barrow itself was neither good nor evil but was, instead, animated by whatever it was that animated the land, the thing that animated each and every one of them and, so, revealed itself in its hiddenness. In fact, one felt, or he felt as he walked – blasphemous though the thought was – that God was only an aspect of the hidden, an idea brought into being by man in order to point to a deeper thing that had no name and reigned beyond silence.

For an instant as he walked from Petersen's gravel pit to St. Mary's rectory, Christopher Pennant was vertiginously pagan and in touch with the hiddenness that coursed through him *and* his God.

Naturally, he kept these thoughts and feelings to himself.

IV

JULY, AUGUST AND AFTER

Jane had spent Barrow Day alone, for the most part. She'd watched the revellers from inside her parents' house, ashamed of what she took to be the town's puerile ways. Barrow Day was an embarrassment and for a number of years now she had taken to spending June 15th at home, usually alone, usually with a book.

This year, she read *Breakfast at Tiffany's* for the fourth time and dreamed of New York and London, Paris and Amsterdam. She almost always enjoyed her solitude, but this year it was charged with something. Something was on its way. Something or someone would come into her life to save her from the louts and boors of Barrow. She could feel it. She sat in the living room, in a chair that had been made by her great-grandfather, the floor lamp with its floral shade beside her, the house smelling of Barrow bread, the noise of the world dimmed by closed doors and shut windows. She left the curtains open, however, and from time to time she could see groups of revellers as they passed.

Robbie had refused to walk naked into Atkinson's.

After the fire-hall dinner and dance, Jane's parents returned. They were childishly happy about something. Mrs. Keynes, one of their neighbours, had inhaled an olive pit and had needed the Heimlich to clear her windpipe. That wasn't the amusing part. What was amusing was the sight of Mr. Chester, a man thin as a whippet and half Dora Keynes's size, trying desperately to squeeze Dora's 'thorax' (her mother's word). The definition of futility. Mrs. Keynes had flung him around from side to side in her struggles for breath, until Jane's father snuck up behind her and, with poor Mr. Chester between them, squeezed the olive out of the exhausted woman.

– Shucks, it was nothing, said her father, smirking.

– It was too, said her mother. And it's too bad you weren't there, Jane. You should come out to Petersen's tonight. It wouldn't hurt you to be sociable and maybe meet someone other than Robbie Myers.

– Mom, my private life's none of your business, said Jane.

– It's my business when everybody in town is talking about my daughter like she's a scarlet woman.

– No, said Jane. It's not your business. And who cares what other people are saying?

– Well, just remember, said her father, don't go kissin' by the garden gate. 'Cause love is blind but the neighbours ain't.

Exasperated by her giggling parents, Jane got up and, with a show of annoyance, flounced from the room. Her mother's words stayed with her, though.

– *It wouldn't hurt you to be sociable and maybe meet someone other than Robbie Myers.*

The words made her want to see Robbie. So, shortly after her parents left for the gravel pit, Jane took a flashlight and went out to Petersen's on her own.

The sky was clear. There were a trillion stars and it was warm enough that her sweater was too much. She took it off, tied it around her waist and then found she was cold. After a brief battle with herself, she hung the sweater from her shoulders. Once out of town, it was as if she disappeared. The group of people in front of her was jovial and paid her no attention. The group behind was much the same. She was alone without being alone.

The sky, the stars, the night, the trees; the world a collection of simple things, from the smell of pine to the stridulating crickets. She should have found the night consoling, but it was all rustic and empty to her: nothing for anyone but the lovers of nothing.

At Petersen's gate, Jane turned off her flashlight and followed the revellers. The place smelled of earth and standing water. Above the trees you could see a handful of stars and then, as they came to the clearing, the sky was grand again, filled with suns that warmed countless other worlds. Jane heard voices she recognized but no one she wanted to talk to. From time to time, light from candles or torches lit her, almost inviting her to take part in the celebrations, but she kept to the edge of the crowd, looking away whenever she thought anyone might be looking at her.

Against the odds, what with the faces of her fellow citizens only partially revealed by the shimmering light, she saw Robbie. He was in the second row of spectators on one side of the pit. She recognized him and then imagined she heard his voice as she saw his lips move. Beside him: Elizabeth, the one who belonged. Despite herself, Jane felt betrayed. Though she wanted to leave Barrow, she resented Elizabeth Denny's acceptance here. An orphan, imagine that, a come-from-away, and yet there was place for Liz Denny and none for her.

There was a hush and then the sound of Mayor Fox reciting gibberish as he walked across the water. Big deal. A cheap, ridiculous trick. And to hear the in-drawn breath of four hundred bumpkins! To think this was Barrow's idea of ceremony. It was a meaningless end to a meaningless day, meaningless years, meaningless lives. To hell with Barrow, she thought, and left the gravel pit before the mayor had made it halfway across.

Jane walked back home alone, the beam of her flashlight like a ground-sniffing dog before her. How had she failed to convince Robbie? Could it be that Elizabeth Denny actually knew him better than she did? Jane had waited until he was most vulnerable. She had arranged things perfectly. On a night when her parents were away, she had invited him over, fed him his favourite meal (shepherd's pie) and seduced him.

Afterwards, in her bed, she had asked

– Robbie, how much do you love me?

– I love you as much as I can love anyone, he'd answered.

– What would you do for me?

– Anything you want, except I won't give Lizzie up.

– But anything but that?

He had cheered up then, the bastard, since he didn't have to give up his 'wife.'

– What do you want me to do? he'd asked. Name it.

As if rummaging in her mind for a suitable task, she'd taken a minute before asking

– Would you take your clothes off in public?

as if the thought had just occurred to her.

He'd been lying up in bed, turned toward her, smiling. But the smile had stuck on his face at the question. He hadn't known what to say. Perhaps thinking it was a joke, he'd answered

– Of course I would.

– I'm serious, she'd said. I want you to show me how much you love me. I want you to walk into Atkinson's Beauty Parlour naked.

Robbie had stared at her and then laughed.

– Sure, he'd said. I'll go into Atkinson's naked. Why not?

– That's wonderful. Why don't you do it tomorrow?

She had kissed him and they had spent the night in each other's arms, though his snoring had kept her up until two in the morning. But when day came and she reminded him of his promise, he had tried to laugh it off. She'd pressed him on it. He'd tried to avoid the subject until, finally, he'd refused outright. He wouldn't do it in a million years was his new tack. He hadn't been serious the night before. He simply wouldn't do it. If she wanted proof of his affection, he'd rather jump to his death.

— But you've got nothing to be ashamed of. What are you worried about?

It was true. He had nothing to be ashamed of. The ladies having their hair done would see a well-built man. No one would object on that score. But there was no talking him into it. In fact, though they had planned to spend the day together, he had walked out, angry at her pestering. That had been a surprise. She'd been so certain she could get him to do anything she asked. She hadn't bothered to think things through or devise another approach. She had failed, and the more she thought about it, the more she felt ridiculous.

As she walked home at the end of Barrow Day, she felt helpless.

Then it occurred to Jane that she'd been cowardly. Yes, cowardly. The stakes were not as high for her as they were for dowdy, four-eyed Elizabeth. Elizabeth stood to lose someone who mattered to her. But she, Jane, was not as attached to Robbie. What then had she really stood to lose? Nothing. For her to truly care if Robbie went into Atkinson's or not, for her to be persuasive, the stake had to be more significant. So, beneath the stars, Jane resolved that should she fail to convince Robbie to do what she asked, she would leave Barrow for good. She would leave everyone and everything she knew behind. A fleetingly painful thought, because something deep within her wanted to be part of Barrow or, at least, wanted to belong somewhere.

As she was superstitious (a trait she shared with most everyone in Barrow), Jane consulted *The Book of Common Prayer* as soon as she got home. She had been doing this all her life, whenever she had to make an important decision: opening the prayer book to a page chosen at random, trusting that the first words she encountered would have some bearing on her decision.

She inevitably used the ancient *Book of Common Prayer* her parents kept in a locked cabinet in the living room. The book, a first edition from the eighteenth century, was bound in thick brown leather that was cracked and scored. The prayer book's pages were brittle, its print looking more like handwriting than anything from a printing press. An heirloom, it had once belonged to her grandfather's grandmother. But Jane was not afraid to touch the book, to use it to guide her. For instance, when she had been wondering if she should go out with Robbie, she had opened the book to a prayer about love and she had taken that to mean that, yes, she and Robbie belonged together. She unlocked the cabinet and took the heavy book from its place. It smelled of Time itself. That is, when Jane thought about Time or History, the thought conjured this smell: dust, dry pages, desiccated leather.

Closing her eyes and thinking of a question

– Should I leave Barrow if Robbie won't do what I ask?

Jane opened the book, put her finger down on a line and, opening her eyes, read

In the Lord I put my trust; how say you to my soul, Flee as a bird to your mountain?

The meaning was obscure, but Jane resisted the urge to see where the words came from. She read the phrase over and over, allowing it to sink into her imagination. Then she closed the prayer book and locked it away again.

In the Lord I put my trust … Flee as a bird to your mountain?

As she got ready for bed, the words nestled in her mind and then, just before she fell asleep, they bloomed. She imagined herself flying, eyes closed, toward a city, a mountain of glass and light. Before the first wave of dreams buried her under a million symbols, she felt certain she'd made the right decision. If Robbie did not do as she asked, she would flee from Barrow. *The Book of Common Prayer* advised it.

At the end of Barrow Day, after watching Mayor Fox, Father Pennant experienced the curious sensation of falling that had preceded his decision to be a priest.

Christopher Pennant was born in Ottawa, but his family had property in Cumberland. Ottawa had been home, but Cumberland was where they had spent their summers, at a cottage where he could be close to his parents, brothers and sisters without thinking about much or worrying about anything.

Cumberland, with its fields and stones, was where he had his first religious feelings. The very first of these he remembered clearly. It had been a warm day in August, with dark clouds wriggling over the blue sky. He and his brothers and sisters were all inside, where it was humid and smelled of paint. Every once in a while, the screen door to the kitchen clacked, as his father went out to check the meat cooking on the barbecue, and every now and then the smell of burning charcoal and hamburger would pass through the cottage.

He hadn't been doing much: idly playing with an old deck of cards, by himself because everyone else had tired of crazy eights and old maid. He could recall the cards still: their red backing curled up at the edges to reveal the white pith between the lamination and the surface. He had just arranged the cards for a game of solitaire when he heard his name called:

– Christopher.

– Yes? he'd answered.

But when he looked around to see who had called, there was no one with him. Everyone else had left for other parts of the cottage or gone outside.

In retrospect, it was surprising how little fear he'd felt. The voice had sounded playful. Then he heard his name again. This time it seemed to come from the kitchen, so he got up to see who it was. As he entered the kitchen, time, as they say, stood still. He heard nothing, neither the hum and creak of the cottage, nor the distant voices of his family. He seemed to be alone in the world when, suddenly, his solitude dissolved (or modulated) into the most intense feeling of company. Far from feeling alone, he felt whole, as if he himself were the cottage and the field behind it, the green hill in the distance and the roiling clouds above. For what seemed like hours, his ten-year-old self stared out the window at the sky and the fields as if he were staring at his own face in a mirror. As suddenly as the feeling had come, it dissipated. His father came into the kitchen. The screen door clacked and the world returned to him, like a stream flowing over an obstruction.

Though he was too young to fully understand the implications of a call, ten-year-old Christopher instinctively knew that the voice that had called his name belonged to the Lord. He was certain of it.

Doubt came fifteen years later when he entered the seminary to become a priest. Most of his fellow seminarians experienced similar doubts, but their doubts were generally about their own fitness to serve God. Most of them worried they were not pure enough. Some worried the Church was not pure enough. Still others began to question the nature or even the existence of God. Christopher Pennant was closest to this third group.

While he was a seminarian, his doubt centred on a question that he had not previously conceived of, let alone resolved: who, exactly, had called his name that day in Cumberland? Had he been too quick to accept that the voice belonged to God? If it had not been the voice of God, whose voice had it been? Did his teachers not insist that Satan's voice is sweet? For a terrible moment at the seminary, it was as if he had been living a lie. (And what could it mean to confuse His voice and the voice of His shadow?)

So, at the threshold of priesthood, he faltered.

But then, influenced by his fellow seminarians, he again came to believe that the voice calling him had been God's. Satan, they said (as if they had all been acquainted with Satan), would have led him on a different course. He, Christopher Thomas Pennant, would not have chosen the church if Satan had called to him. Gradually, Father Pennant's doubts were quelled. His crisis passed.

What Lowther could not have known was that Father Pennant's encounter with 'evil' (or, more exactly, with Mayor Fox) would precipitate a return to the uncertainty that had lain unexamined within him since the end of his time at seminary. Watching Mayor Fox walk on water had, metaphorically speaking, plunged him into a tide of questions. Who had called him? Whose voice had he heard? To whom was his vocation dedicated?

At seminary, Christopher had struggled because he had not known if the voice he'd heard belonged to God or Satan. Following Barrow Day, a new thought occurred to him. What if it had been neither God nor Satan? What if it had been the land itself that had called him? What if it had been Cumberland – the hills, the trees, the stony fields – that spoke? If so, could one serve both God *and* the land? Were they indistinguishable or were they, rather, two jealous masters, only one of whom could be devoutly followed?

These feelings were in themselves enough to shake him up, but they were accompanied by a coldness, a critical eye on God's habits. Take the matter of miracles, for instance. Looking back on Heath Lambert's gypsy moths, Father Pennant – though he did not know what Lambert had done to the insects or how he had got them to fly in a circle – suddenly felt the too-muchness of 'miracles.' Not that the thing with moths had been miraculous, but it was just the kind of thing God might do: ostentatiously contravene the laws of Nature. The Lord was showy when called upon to prove himself: He made bushes speak, He parted the seas, He restored sight to the blind. Honestly, making moths do His bidding was very like Him.

After Barrow Day, Father Pennant began to reconsider the question that had troubled him at the seminary. He did not feel the same dismay, however. He felt apprehensive, but he was also intrigued. Caught up with his journals and his accounts of the natural history of Barrow, he did not mind the idea that the land had once called to him, or that he was on intimate terms with Nature. As a result, Father Pennant began to spend even more time exploring the fields and streams of Lambton County. He performed his priestly duties and performed them well, but he was now distracted. His sermons grew short and to the point. His visits to the sick were efficiently carried out, and his attendance at spiritual gatherings was thoughtful, not enthusiastic.

Barrow Day done, the town settled into the routines of summer: preparing for vacation and looking forward to weekends up near Goderich.

Robbie Myers, who believed he was in the clear with both of the women he loved, was happily occupied with work on the farm, with his friends, with the question of whether or not he should invite Jane to his wedding. Barrow Day had been good. He'd spent it with Elizabeth who, though she was not her affectionate self, spoke to him without rancour and even, once or twice, held his hand. It was sad that she would not allow him to touch her in any intimate way and that her kisses were perfunctory. But she still wanted to marry him and she treated him – as far as others were concerned – the way you would expect a woman to treat her fiancé. He was convinced that the Elizabeth he loved would return to him once she realized how much he loved her. But for an argument with Jane over some strange idea she'd got in her head – something to do with him committing public indecency – all was right with the world.

Then, four days after the 15th, Jane invited him over and coolly gave him an ultimatum: he was to walk naked into Atkinson's Hair Salon or she would leave town.

Once he accepted that Jane might really leave, Robbie panicked. The ultimatum was absurd. It made no sense, except as some torment or prank. Why should anyone – let alone Jane – want him to expose himself to a clutch of older women? It was like asking a man afraid of rats to snuggle into a tub full of them. His fear of public nudity was irrational and unmanageable.

Then again, so were his feelings for Jane. He loved her as much as he said he did. He could have easily done almost anything for her, easily done anything but this.

– I need to know what you're going to do, Jane said.

– Can't I think about it?

– No. I want to know right now.

Robbie was not used to thinking and he was not good at it. Under pressure, what came was confusion: feelings, not thoughts; pictures, not words. He felt humiliation, longing, fear. He saw Jane's face, the red birth stain on his chest, his mother's face, the entrance to Atkinson's Beauty Parlour. No single feeling or picture was distinct.

But then, because he was the man he was, one strong thing came out of the confusion: love. 'Love' had caused him trouble in the recent past, but he went with it anyway, stubbornly holding to the idea that 'love' – whenever and wherever it touched down – was always right.

– Okay, he said. I'll do it if I have to.

It was an acquiescence that surprised them both.

– Oh, said Jane, her tone very like one of disappointment. That's ... great.

She kissed him, but she was not happy. She had, she realized, been expecting him to say no. She had unconsciously put her faith in Elizabeth's knowledge of him. Not that her kiss or the emotion behind it registered with Robbie. The man was shocked by his own decision.

– When do I have to do this? he asked.

– Do it tomorrow, said Jane. It's Friday. It'll be busy.

But it wasn't the number of people that mattered to Robbie. He would have been as terrified at the thought of one witness as he was at the thought of thousands.

– I'm doing this because I love you, he said.

– You can change your mind, answered Jane.

He did not, though it felt as if he had agreed to his own execution. For a moment Jane wondered if she weren't being cruel. But then, the cruelty was Elizabeth's, wasn't it? She herself would not have dreamed such a humiliation. It would not have bothered her in the least to walk around town naked, so part of her was unsympathetic to Robbie's plight. Still, at the thought of Elizabeth's wager, Jane began to wonder if Liz weren't more bitter and vindictive than she let on.

For Robbie, the following morning came after a night of fitful sleep. He'd suffered through countless visions of himself walking naked along the streets of Barrow. Oddly, the one place he did not dream of was Atkinson's. He dreamed he was naked in church, naked in school, naked in the Blackhawk Tavern. He tried to convince himself that his fear was irrational and, so, ridiculous. He told himself that human beings were born naked, that nudity was not traumatic for him in most situations. Nothing helped. He did not want to walk into Atkinson's naked. He could not understand why this was important to Jane. He thought about whether or not he loved her enough to do this, but, sadly, the answer was yes. It was always yes, like rolling the dice over and over and coming up snake eyes forever. He also considered avoiding this one thing, making it up to Jane in other ways if he could. But Jane was not a person whose resolve needed testing. She had assured him she would leave if he did not go into Atkinson's and he knew, knew for certain, that she would keep her word. He was a condemned man.

Once he'd finished his chores, he ate breakfast as if it were to be his last: porridge and maple syrup followed by a glass of his mother's dandelion wine.

Catching him with the wine, his mother was alarmed.

– What's the matter with you? she asked. You know I need that for knitting circle.

Robbie apologized and put the cork back in the bottle. Rather than replace the bottle on its rack in the winter closet, though, he carried it into the barn and finished it off, disturbing a couple of mice in the straw. Dutch courage, people called it, though no one could tell him why the Dutch should be known for such a sensible way of dealing with distress. *He* thought it sensible, anyway. What else could you do but drink or pray?

– Father, if it be thy will, let this cup pass from me ...

Drink or pray, however, there was no getting around his anxiety. He resolved to go into Atkinson's early in the day. The place opened at ten. Waiting for noon or for the end of the day would have driven him squirrelly. So, at ten o'clock in the morning, having downed a bottle of his mother's sickly sweet wine, Robbie went with a neighbour into Barrow, getting out at Barrow Park.

There were, naturally, things that Robbie hadn't considered. Where to undress, for instance? Where to put his clothes once he'd undressed? Too inebriated to drive to town alone, he could not put them in his truck. Could he leave his shoes on or did 'naked' mean entirely naked? He supposed he could leave his shoes on until just before he entered the parlour and that is what he did. With no word to anyone around him and as if it were a thing people always did, Robbie stood up when the clock at city hall struck half past ten, took off his shoes, removed his clothes, then put his shoes on again. Being slightly drunk, he undressed deliberately, with exaggerated precision. He then walked, his clothes under one arm, from the park to the beauty parlour, some two minutes away. The walk, the experience of it, was what others might have called otherworldly. It was as if his anxiety had taken on a form of its own and was walking with him, a sensation so odd Robbie felt almost relaxed. And perhaps because Robbie appeared to be at ease, few of the half dozen or so people who were about noticed him.

One woman, just coming home from a shift at Dow Chemical, did notice Robbie was naked, but there was a delay in her perception. She saw Robbie and walked by him. Then, as if out of nowhere, a thought occurred to her:

– You know, I've seen very few penises besides Michael's.

It was only then that she realized – to her dismay – that she had just seen Robbie Myers naked. By which time Robbie had entered Atkinson's.

Inside the beauty parlour, there were three older women: Emma Cavendish, Leda Preston and Margaret Burke. The three women, all in their late sixties or early seventies, all spry, had their hair done once a month. They inevitably went together, and had been doing so for years. This was their day. They had left their homes early, eaten poached eggs and toast at Boucher's Diner and presented themselves to Agnes Atkinson at twenty after ten.

Clouds had been gathering since early morning and Leda said
– I think it's going to rain.

The women instinctively turned to the glass door to look outside.
– Is there someone trying to get in? Emma asked.

– I think there is, said Margaret.

As she spoke, the door opened and Robbie Myers walked in.

– Goodness, said Margaret. Is it raining already?

All turned to Robbie. Agnes, who knew him best, though they all knew him, said

– Robert, put your clothes on. What would your mother think?

– His clothes! said Leda. I thought there was something missing.

– The library's just down the street, said Emma.

A curiously apposite non sequitur. Emma's friends mumbled in agreement. At which point Robbie, thrown from his trance, was suddenly aware of his situation. He wanted nothing so much as to flee. It took almost superhuman resolve to put his clothes on carefully and to dress without throwing up. Once he began to dress, the women seemed to lose interest in him. Agnes did ask if everything was all right, but she turned away to devote herself to washing Emma's hair. The older women, as bewildered by Emma's comment as Robbie's behaviour, began a conversation about libraries and modern morals.

Dressed, Robbie apologized.

– It's awfully early to be drinking, said Agnes. I'm afraid I'm going to have to tell your mother about this.

As if he were still a boy, Robbie said

– I'm sorry, Mrs. Atkinson

and walked out into what was now a light, warm rain.

For all the attention paid the matter while Robbie was in Atkinson's, a stranger might have wondered if Barrow's young men did not habitually go naked into beauty parlours. But as it is with so many unusual moments, the incident grew in the imaginations of those who had lived it. It became more significant the more they were asked about it. What had they seen? (Well, everything!) Did they know why Robbie had come into the parlour like that? (He was drunk!) Was he really drunk, or is it something worse, because, you know, there's been insanity in the Myers family before? (So true! They hid Robbie's uncle Mark away for ages, before they put him in a proper home. Robbie's most likely the same way. Just think what'll happen if Liz Denny has kids with that boy!)

The more anyone thought about it, the more peculiar it became: slightly sinister for some, amusing for others. Still, as nothing dangerously wrong had happened and as Robbie's subsequent attitude – contrite, embarrassed – was not alarming, the incident was blamed on alcohol and forgotten a relatively short time later. (That is, it was never forgotten, but, after a certain time, it was only ever brought up in jest.)

Jane was angry that Robbie had done what she'd asked.

Elizabeth was humiliated, or *further* humiliated, because Robbie's humiliation was hers too: yet another dose of misery. People began to openly wonder if he was a suitable husband for any self-respecting woman, and they all felt compelled to tell her so. The general consensus was that Elizabeth had good reason to back out of the wedding.

A few days after Robbie scandalized the women in Atkinson's, Elizabeth and Jane met in St. Mary's. They spoke quietly near the front of the church while a handful of sinners waited to confess at the back. The day was dark. The rain came down in a pale, earth-lit shower. Thunder sounded in the distance, as if the land were clearing its throat every so often. It was a relief to enter the church, though the interior was gloomy and the stained-glass saints, their colours darkened, lost much of their charm. The light inside was as thin as if it were shining through khaki cloth.

Without a hint of triumph, Jane said

– I told you this would happen.

– I know that, answered Elizabeth. I'm sorry I asked you to do it.

– You should have thought about that before you asked.

– You don't have to go on about it.

The wind outside sounded like distant, tuneless whistling. For a moment, the two women sat quietly, staring at the altar while listening to the storm, to the whispers from the confessional, to the crepitations of the church itself as it withstood the weather.

— I told you, Jane repeated, there isn't anything I can't get Robbie to do.

Above all, Elizabeth hated the sound of the woman's voice. Jane Richardson was unbearable, but it was she herself who had chosen this road. What could she say? At least the question of her marriage had been decided.

— There's nothing else to say, said Elizabeth. I hope you and Robbie are happy together.

Jane felt guilt and alarm.

— I told you, she repeated

then stopped herself. It all suddenly seemed like some kind of joke. But at whose expense?

Thunder rattled the church and rain now thrummed against the stained glass. It was oppressively humid and, inside, mixed in with the smell of incense, was a strong whiff of rot. Elizabeth rose from the pew and said, with more bitterness than she'd intended

— I hope I never have to see your face again.

— That makes two of us, said Jane.

Elizabeth walked to the back of the church, to the confessional. There was much on her mind. Her wedding, for instance. She should have postponed it, given the circumstances, but she had gone on with the planning and the arrangements. She had chosen a wedding dress. And although they had not had sex for months now, she had gone on seeing Robbie, nursing what was left of her feelings for him.

How much she wanted Robbie punished, and how much she wanted Jane Richardson hurt! For the first time in her life, she felt hatred, and was upset at how intimate hatred was. She had said that she hoped never to see Jane Richardson again. That was true, but it was also true that a part of her wanted Jane Richardson near her always. She felt a physical longing to damage the woman, to hit, to bite, to grind her into the dust. These feelings, close as they were to desire, were the hardest to bear, and they were the ones for which she felt shame.

Once its thick velvet curtains were drawn together, the confessional was dark. The sounds of the church and the noise of the storm were muffled to a rumour. When Father Pennant opened the grilled partition between his face and hers she could immediately smell the mint he used for his breath. She hoped her own breath was not sour. She had intended to confess her anger and hatred, but in the confessional she found she could not. However much she wanted to, she could not speak of anything true.

– Bless me, Father, for I have sinned. It has been two months since my last confession. Since then I've ... been disrespectful to my parents and I've ...

She received forgiveness for a handful of petty – or invented – misdemeanours.

– Go, my child, and sin no more.
And left feeling as if she had betrayed herself.

The episode at Atkinson's was humiliating for Robbie, but not because he'd been naked. The look on Agnes Atkinson's face – embarrassed, peeved, maternal – was a source of pain whenever he remembered it. And then Agnes had complained to his mother and, worse yet, his mother had felt compelled to speak to him about it.

– I've been hearing strange things from Agnes Atkinson, Robbie. Now, you're old enough for me to speak to you like a man and I shouldn't have to tell you, you shouldn't be exposing yourself to women. Don't interrupt. I understand you might be thinking it's not as bad, you exposing yourself to older women. Most young men, they think older women don't have feelings, but we do. And it's bad enough the women in Atkinson's have to see you in your birthday suit, but did you even think about what Elizabeth's going through? How's she supposed to hold her head up with her fiancé embarrassing himself all over town? Don't you dare interrupt, Robert. There's nothing you can say about this. Your father's convinced this is some stupid dare. One of the Bigland boys dared you, didn't they? Don't interrupt. You don't have to tell me anything. I don't want to hear your explanation. I want you to promise you won't be doing this kind of thing again. Barrow isn't the place for these shenanigans. You need to move to Sarnia if you're going to expose yourself like that. Sarnia's too big for anyone to know anyone else. No one cares about anything there. You and those damned Bigland boys should move to Sarnia and not ruin things for people in Barrow. Honestly, I don't know why Elizabeth has stuck with you. You should thank your stars. And that's the last I'm going to say about all this. You understand? I want you to promise this isn't going to happen again and then we'll drop the subject. You understand?

He had, of course, promised, because he did not want to talk about this with his mother any more than she wanted to talk about it with him. Still, the humiliation and embarrassment were things one might have expected to feel after traipsing around in one's altogethers. The strange thing, the thing he could not have predicted, was the exhilaration he'd been feeling since walking out of the beauty parlour. He had faced his greatest fear and he had overcome it. He had done all that for Jane. How much he loved her! He had never loved anyone like this, maybe not even Liz.

He did not want to repeat the experience, it's true, but he now knew what it was to love someone beyond what he'd thought possible. Though he could not understand why Jane had asked him to walk into Atkinson's, he would be grateful to her for the rest of his life. Days after his mother had chewed him out for acting foolishly, he felt more willing than ever to follow where Jane led. What a woman she was! He would never leave her.

And, again: was he not marrying the wrong woman?

Wasn't this feeling, the exhilaration of submission, what marriage was all about?

For generations, the men in Lowther's family had been dying at the age of sixty-three. Lowther's father, grandfather, great-grandfather . . .

all the way back to at least seven times great. It was taken by most in his family to be a curse. Lowther's mother had seen it that way, as had his father. But Lowther took the matter differently. He took it as a promise, God's word.

He hadn't always faced his 'pre-ordained' death with equanimity. As a younger man, he had been defiant, angry. Knowing he would die at the age of sixty-three gave Lowther, when he was younger, a disregard for his life.

Of course, his early attitude had something to do with the moment he learned that his time on earth was fixed. On Lowther's twelfth birthday, his father, drunk and lugubrious, had taken him aside and let him in on his fate. Mr. Williams, going through a spiritual crisis, had wept and then apologized for having passed on a death sentence. What had impressed and traumatized the young Lowther was not the age at which he was to die. As for any twelve-year-old, sixty-three seemed ancient verging on unreachable. At twelve, he himself might have chosen a more reasonable age at which to go: thirty-five, say, or fifty at the outside. It was the spectacle of his drunken father and the fact of his father's certainty (a certainty that proved well-founded), his father's conviction that this was an injustice handed down to them from God Himself. The Williamses, in other words, were cursed by a God whose attention they had, though they could not put it to good effect.

It was no doubt sad that his days were so specific in number, thought Lowther, but the opposite side of the coin was: he would not die *until* he was sixty-three. If God's word was true, Lowther had been given licence to do whatever he liked until then.

His twenties and thirties were filled with a recklessness that would have made most men blanch. He went in search of danger to test his destiny. He did the usual jumping from planes and tall cliffs. He worked in the jungles of South America, handled poisonous snakes as a member of a cult in rural Georgia, and travelled to the most unfriendly parts of the world, in pursuit of death. As a result, he and death were on familiar terms long before his sixty-third birthday. By the age of forty, Lowther had seen men, women and children shot, stabbed, run over, thrown from high windows, set alight. He had seen a severed human hand still holding a cigarette, the head of a woman, eyes open, thrown into a shallow hole in a dirt path and a newborn child nailed to a tree. The death of others meant little to him.

When Lowther was in his forties, his father died of liver cancer. It took a year, a year during which Mr. Williams longed for a death that would not come. Whenever they spoke, his father was either gone on morphine, drifting in and out of consciousness, or lucid enough to feel bitter that the cancer had pounced on him somewhere around his sixty-second birthday, leaving him with a year to suffer. As his sixty-third birthday approached, however, knowing that his death was coming at last, Lowther's father held his son's hand and apologized for what he'd passed on. Lowther saw his father off on the morning of May 4th, as a robin sang and a breeze came through an open window. It was the morning of his father's sixty-third birthday. The inevitable was inevitable, after all.

As father and son had both expected the end to come around the time it did, his father's death could not be said to have drastically changed Lowther's view of life. It had been eerie to have the thing arrive so tightly to schedule, but the death that changed him for good came *after* his father had passed.

While working as a skip tracer, Lowther had tracked down a man who had fallen seriously behind on the payments for an El Dorado. It was Lowther's duty to get either the money owed or the car. He came to an elegant, red-brick house in Sarnia, not far from the river. A good address in a good neighbourhood, but the front lawn needed mowing, and rose bushes in the garden had withered, their petals scattered on the dirt. Lowther imagined that the man he sought had once been wealthy and, even on the run from debtors, could not do without the trappings of success. Everything about him seemed to confirm it: seedy clothes that had once been fine, good grooming, even a kind of annoyed politeness when Lowther explained his business. In fact, his only words to Lowther were spoken with a hint of largesse.

– Fine, he said, do come in.

Inside the house was a different matter. The living room into which Lowther stepped had only one piece of furniture: a reclining, faux-leather armchair. But the place was in disarray. Old newspapers everywhere, plates stacked on the floor, knives and forks here and there, here and there children's clothing and countless toys. Lowther had taken the place in and was standing near the alcove when the man came back carrying a five-year-old boy and a revolver. Lowther felt surprise, not panic, not fear. He had been threatened more often than he could remember, but always by a certain type – men or women whose demons were not well-hidden. The man put the child, who was eating an arrowroot cookie, down on the floor. The child looked blankly Lowther's way before the man, looking at Lowther, shot the boy in the back of the head. He then turned the revolver on himself, shooting himself in the face.

If you had asked Lowther, at that moment, what he felt, he would have said curiosity, the kind of curiosity one feels about a puzzle of some sort or a riddle whose answer was just beyond one's ken. From his perspective, a predictable sequence of events had been followed by an outcome that made no sense: two bodies on the floor, blood on the walls and on Lowther's brown shoes. A small, intimate massacre staged for him alone, it seemed. He had witnessed worse, but not with his guard down. He had been defenceless. Curiosity remained his chief emotion as he called the police, waited in the house for them, told them what had happened and then gone to the police station to tell everything again.

On his own, Lowther tried to dig deeper. The man who'd killed himself and his son had lost all his money in some business deal, had been left by his wife, had come to the end of his rope. Why hadn't he shot Lowther? Why had he killed his son? To punish his wife? To punish himself? To punish Lowther? Impossible to answer any of these questions without resorting to banalities like 'fate.' There was something missing, somewhere. Lowther ate, slept, drank, lived on, carried on with his work for weeks, like a man only slightly unhinged.

Then, one day, apropos of nothing, he remembered the look in the man's eyes. Pure nothingness, an abyss. That look, that abyss, was like a bell in Lowther's consciousness, its one note endlessly sounding. A month after he'd witnessed the small massacre, Lowther abandoned the life he had been living. He did not simply change jobs. He withdrew from the world he had known. Having found a point beyond which he could not go, having encountered the abyss in another man, Lowther 'woke up.' There were still some twenty years before his sixty-third birthday. He decided to spend them studying life, leaving death to its own devices.

In the beginning, it was not easy to tell how best to study life. He read all he could about all manner of things and finally came away with the idea of submission, submission to the world. He resolved to be attentive to things others largely ignored. He studied mycology and entomology. He could walk in the woods and reliably identify which mushrooms were safe to eat. He could name endless species of beetles, flies, ants and spiders. He also knew his trees and birds well. After a while, birdsong became as coherent as the cries, voices, whispers and laughter one hears when humans congregate. For the sheer discipline of it, he taught himself to cook. And he resolved to master the cello when, one day, he heard a passionate woman playing a sonata by Debussy. By the time he met Father Pennant, he had been playing the cello two hours a day for twenty years.

None of his obligations – his time with the cello, his study of small things – was obsessively carried out. He listened and looked and, in the process, kept himself open to the world. His decision to work for Father Fowler was based on happenstance. He'd been walking around Barrow one afternoon when it began to rain. He had thought to take shelter in St. Mary's church, but it was locked. Lowther had turned away when he noticed two white bowls on the church steps, the water in them clear, dimpled by rainfall. Water so clear it made him thirsty. Having paused to admire the white bowls, he was about to walk away when one of the doors opened and Father Fowler looked out.

– Come in, said the priest. You'll catch your death out there. Would you mind picking the bowls up? I put out milk for the strays. Poor things.

Over the years, Lowther had got to know Father Fowler well and, as time passed, it seemed to him that Father Fowler was honourable. Having decided the priest was a good man, he was determined to have Father Fowler shepherd him through his – that is Lowther's – death. So, when Father Fowler died before him, he was saddened to lose his friend as well as his guide.

But what did it matter who gave him extreme unction?

It mattered to Lowther the way correctly playing a piece by Bach or Debussy mattered. Not flawlessly in the sense of getting every note and notation right. That kind of flawless happened rarely, but its occurrence was trivial. In fact, when all the notes and tempi, trills and pizzicati were rightly hit, it usually meant he had been thinking about notes and tempi, trills and pizzicati, not about music. As he slowly discovered over years of listening and playing, music was an affair of spirit and moment. And that was it: he wished his final moments on earth to be musical, an offering from one world to the next. Death would come, no matter what, but he wished to accomplish it with spirit and grace. And these qualities, if they were to be had at all with a priest, called for the right priest, a man without pretension or falseness of spirit.

Father Fowler had been just the man. So, his death had been a setback. But then Father Pennant had come and, with Heath's help, Lowther had tested him, had devised a 'miracle' to see how the man would react. As far as Lowther was concerned, Christopher Pennant was just the shepherd he wanted: modest, thoughtful, curious about the world and, much as Father Fowler had been, a lover of music and a man with a sensibility. With Father Pennant there, Lowther was convinced his death would be a proper duet.

With that settled, he had only his own soul to worry about. He would confess in order to clear his conscience, give away his possessions in order to unburden and prepare himself to face whatever pain there was to be on the day of his death.

So, two weeks before his sixty-third birthday, Lowther dealt with his possessions. He had been successful and thrifty, so there were hundreds of thousands of dollars to disperse. He had no immediate family. He had chosen not to pass on the Williams curse. He wrote a will, bequeathing all his money and his cello to Father Pennant. Lowther owned a house in Petrolia. He left it to the family who had been renting it for the past decade. He had a house in Sarnia. He left this to the mother of the child whose murder he had witnessed. Not because he felt the death had been his fault, but because he wished to do something for a woman whose suffering had influenced the change in his life.

At the end of July, over the space of three evenings, Lowther confessed his sins to Father Pennant. He painstakingly unveiled his life, thinking it crucial that Father Pennant should know him as he had actually been. Everything of which Lowther was ashamed or proud, his sins and good works, all the details of the man who was Lowther Williams, were laid before the priest who, by the end of the third evening, knew Lowther as well as Lowther knew himself. Only after that did Lowther ask for forgiveness.

Now there was only the preparedness for pain. But there was no pain. Not a hint of it. He felt as healthy two days before his sixty-third birthday (on July 31st) as he had ever felt. No, he felt healthier, more at ease than at any other time in his life. Perversely, this made him miserable. He wondered if God had broken His covenant with the Williamses.

Still, the absence of pain was no proof that death was absent. He had often heard of men and women at the peak of health dropping down dead, like puppets whose strings had been cut, all because their times had come. His time would come. He was sure of it. But his sixty-third birthday (August 2nd) came and went, and the worst of it was he did not feel anything but healthy. Seeking some dark diagnosis, he went to a doctor. But the man was entirely optimistic, congratulating him on the state of his health.

— You've got the body of a forty-year-old, the doctor said.

Despite himself, Lowther was offended. The last thing he wanted was the body of a forty-year-old, unless the forty-year-old in question was terminally ill.

He left the doctor's office confused and momentarily rudderless.

The problem, surely, was one of miscalculation. *His* miscalculation. There were 365 days during which he would be sixty-three. God had plenty of time to take him. But Lowther had planned for a death on his birthday, a death such as his father had had. Every moment that succeeded his sixty-third birthday was like leftovers. He played the cello distractedly, waiting for a heart attack or stroke.

Whereas previously Lowther had had something to look forward to (his appointed death), now there was only the unsettling thought that death would not come when it was due. He needed faith – in God, in God's inclination to kill him sooner rather than later. In fact, Father Pennant's initial impression – that there was something not quite Christian about Lowther's religion – was true. Lowther's relationship to God had been personal and more than a little pagan. Now that he was forced to wonder if God would keep His end of the compact, Lowther's feelings were hurt.

Heath and Father Pennant were the ones who bore the brunt of Lowther's unhappiness.

Where, previously, Lowther had been unflappable and slightly mysterious, a good conversationalist with a wide range of knowledge and an expert's eye for things in the natural world, he was now close-mouthed, manifestly disappointed and interested in one subject alone: the date of his death. For Heath, this was very strange indeed. He was filled with an almost distressing ambivalence. For his friend's sake, he wished Lowther dead. For his own sake, he wished him long life. When Lowther was around, Heath was forced to pretend that a being he did not believe in (viz. 'God') was behaving childishly. And when Lowther was not with him, he genuinely did not know if he wanted his closest friend alive or not.

Father Pennant was not convinced that death could be as predictable as Lowther thought it, though he'd felt honoured that

Lowther had chosen him for his confessor. Now, weeks later, Father Pennant was saddened that the man he admired and whose company he treasured was eclipsed by this neurotic sixty-three-year-old who insisted on accompanying him wherever he went: church, Wyoming, the fields around Barrow. Almost everywhere Father Pennant went, Lowther went with him in case there was need for sudden last rites.

It was surprising how quickly this became a burden.

It had been raining for days. A succession of black clouds crawled above Barrow. And what wind! Small things and bits of paper were taken into the air, held, then tossed, as if Lambton County were sullenly looking for something it had lost. Day was as dark as evening, evening as dark as night.

On one of these evenings, Robbie waited for Liz in his room. To create an atmosphere, he had set out slices of Harrington's raisin bread, toasted, on a plate, so that his room smelled of yeast and raisins. Beside the plate, there was a candle in a blue cup: a white candle, some eight inches tall, its wax congealing into perfectly formed droplets along its body.

Liz had asked to see him. No doubt, she had something to say about Atkinson's. Well, she could say what she wanted and he would listen, but he felt he was a better person for having faced his fears and he didn't care when people kidded him about making his short-comings public. Besides, something had shifted in him. He was not as sure as he should have been that he wanted to marry Liz. Feeling as he did now, the right thing would have been to marry Jane.

And yet, the more he thought about how much he wanted Jane, the more vividly images of Liz would come to him: Liz's upper torso, from the bottom of her neck on down, her white robe gaping, most of one breast visible, and her right hand, its long fingers holding the robe closed. A memory like that was imperious, dismissing everything before it. What he would have given to master words! How he wished he could share his feelings with the women he loved.

When Liz knocked at the front door, he let her in and took her up to his room, where the smell of raisin bread had given way to something still yeasty but more burnt. God only knows why she loved this smell, but as it gave her pleasure he did not mind.

The look on her face was impossible to read, and Robbie was suddenly unsure of himself.

– Is everything okay? he asked.

She looked around as if taking the room in for the first time. There was the narrow bed in which they had managed to sleep, side by side, when his parents were away, the coverlet with its blue and white chessboard squares on which there were drawings of the same objects repeated over and again along the white diagonals: a candle, a sheep, bread, a stream, an open book. The walls were light blue, uninterrupted save for the generic painting of a schooner, a painting Mrs. Myers had chosen for the room shortly after Robbie's birth. There was a chest of drawers, a desk that Robbie never used and a bookshelf half-filled with books Robbie had never read: bound copies of *Reader's Digest*, mostly. On the floor there was a crimson-and-red throw rug from somewhere exotic (Iran, his mother said), bought from a Middle Eastern gentleman at a garage sale in Leamington.

– I'm not going to marry you, said Liz.

No one who knew their situation would have been surprised, but Robbie plaintively asked

– Why?

– Where do you want me to start? she said.

A fair question to which there was only one important answer or one true counter-question: did this ending matter to him?

– You know I love you, he said.

– You went into the hairdresser's for Jane. You wouldn't have done that for me.

– Who told you that? It's not true! I didn't do it for Jane! You didn't ask me! I'll do it now if you want.

– No thank you, she answered.

Elizabeth had meant to say all manner of things. She'd meant to remind him of the pain he'd put her through and of her unwavering fidelity. In her imagining of this last moment between them, there was some back and forth: a heartfelt (but too late) apology from him, the assurance that he would never put her through such misery again, the assurance that he would never see Jane Richardson again. In her imagination, this final moment had been something of a quiet triumph. But, in fact, it was all unbearably sad. She felt no more triumph than she would if she had been looking down at a precious vase shattered on a kitchen floor. She hadn't the least interest in his last words. She was finished with him. And yet she still found it difficult to get up from the bed and leave. Leave him, leave the past they shared, leave the future they had planned.

She waited in silence, as Robbie tried to find something appropriate to say.

– But I *do* love you, he said at last.

His one endless note, a note that now turned all her nostalgia and longing to spite.

– I don't love *you*, she said.

And rose to leave.

And then left, there being no words to make her stay.

Robbie had not anticipated this moment. In fact, he had never really thought it possible. When Elizabeth had gone, it seemed to him as if he'd witnessed an accident. Was it his fault that he loved two women at once? Had he asked for such a thing? He had been honest (well, eventually honest), hadn't he? He was a good man in unfortunate circumstances, nothing less. Seeing Liz get up and leave was like the moment immediately after you've bumped into something – a vase, say – and you put your hands out to catch it, only to see it fall (not quite inevitably) to the floor.

Robbie did not think these things. He felt them, obscurely, as if through a fog of other feelings. He had an intuition of loss but ignored it, reassured that, after all, there was Jane, that he could build a life with Jane, that Jane was more exciting than Liz, more likely to bring him unpredictable joys. By the following day, he almost believed that losing Liz was the best thing that could have happened. Love or no love, did he really want the domesticity that went with marriage? No, maybe, never mind. Nevertheless, he'd almost certainly dodged a bullet by avoiding the wrong marriage. Hadn't he?

As soon as he could, Robbie told Jane the good news.

It was, of course, news that Jane knew better than he did. She had been thinking about nothing else since she'd won her wager with Liz Denny. She had also been thinking about the unfortunate deal she'd made with herself. Robbie had done what she'd asked. She had won, so she could not flee to her mountain. She was, if she played by the rules she herself had set, doomed to live in Barrow.

For weeks Jane tried to live honourably, accepting her agreement with herself as a given. She was to live with Robbie Myers? Fine. But she could surely find some way to influence him, to turn him into the kind of man she now knew she wanted. What kind of man was that? Someone who read books, not just magazines. Someone interested in more than cows and sheep. Someone curious about the world outside Lambton County; a man who knew the difference between Paris and La Paz. A man who could entertain her with his wit, not just his muscles and nethers. It wouldn't hurt, either, if he knew a foreign language. French would do, even bad French if he showed ambition to learn. A man who smelled of something other than Ivory soap and Tide detergent. A man whose touch was subtle, one who didn't go at your nipples like taking a bolt off a tractor.

In a word, she was looking for someone other than the man who was now hers.

No surprise: her resolve to remain in Barrow weakened quickly. Knowing the kind of man she wanted, now that she had one she did not want, she soon understood she would never be happy with Robbie. Nor would anyone have blamed her for leaving a man she no longer loved. She did cause 'poor young Myers' some distress before she left, though, in part because she wanted to see if she could change him for the better, in part because she needed to feel

115

the true inanity of a life with Robert before she could find the strength to cut herself permanently off from her roots.

Jane began her experiment with Robbie one rainy night in late summer. They were at her parents' house while her parents were away. She and Robbie had made love, mostly because she'd felt it a duty to sleep with him. Predictably, it hadn't gone well. She'd gotten almost no pleasure out of his exertions and felt only slight gratification when he did. It hadn't been Robbie's fault per se. He did as he always did. That is, he did more or less what she told him to and enjoyed it. But she'd felt empty. Taking up one of several books by the side of her bed, she said

– Why don't we read something together?

– You know I don't read much, he answered.

– I'll read. You listen. It's something we should be doing together if we love each other.

There was nothing you could say to that – her very tone was a warning – so Robbie lay in bed and tried to pay attention. By chance Jane had picked up *Breakfast at Tiffany's*. She showed Robbie the cover.

– Truman Kaput? he asked.

– Ka-*po*-tee, she answered. Haven't you heard of him?

No, of course he hadn't. Worse, she didn't even get to the end of the first section before he fell asleep. The first section? He was snoring by the time she read the words *You heard from Holly?* which were on the second page! Robbie was tired after a day's work, no doubt, but that made no difference to her feelings. She almost cried in frustration.

– Robbie!

– What? What is it?

– You fell asleep before I got to page three!

– I'm sorry. You can start again. I remember something about ... Holly?

Jane began again: *I took a taxi in a downpour of October rain ...*

This time he was asleep by the end of the next paragraph. She threw the book at his head, waking him.

– It's good! he cried out. It's good! I'm liking it!

It was not long after this that their relationship ended.

(On seeing how important *Breakfast at Tiffany's* was for Jane, Robbie did his best to read the novel, letting her know that he really did like it, really. He did not mention that he never got further than the first section, never further than *It was one of these mailboxes that had first made me aware of Holly Golightly*, though he went at the book more than once, starting over each time. Never had he read anything so unmemorable. Here was the best example of what made fiction useless. Who was this 'I' that was talking at him and why should he care what 'I' was saying? It was asking a man a lot, asking him to stick around while someone who had nothing to say said it in the fanciest way possible. He supposed that women liked this sort of thing because they were used to talking. That was the main problem with women, as far as he was concerned. They never could keep quiet. They talked all the time and their intentions were mysterious. Not mysterious in a good way either, like when Phil Bigland had once mentioned 'the infinite' [*a black moth in a black room on a starless, moonless night*, he'd called it] and they had all been quiet out of respect for something deep. No, sir. Womanish mystery was the kind that filled you with dread, not reverence.)

In a roundabout way, Elizabeth was responsible for their breakup. Jane had been trying to instill 'culture' in Robbie, which was like trying to get ten pounds of rice into a two-pound bag. Then, one afternoon, she happened to be passing Harrington's – on the opposite side of the street, of course – and saw Elizabeth Denny shaking crumbs onto the street for the birds. Had Elizabeth seen her? Jane did not know, but she would have sworn there was an ironic look on the woman's face, a look that said

– *You only think you won. I'm the one who gets to do what she wants. I'm free. You're tied to that good-for-nothing dairy farmer who wouldn't know his ass from his elbow. How stupid do you have to be not to see that this is what I wanted all along?*

Jane was incensed at the unfairness of it. She'd been duped. She was sure of it. Duped into abandoning her dreams and aspirations. The humiliation was hard to take. As she watched Elizabeth Denny blithely turn her back and enter the bakery, Jane's futile efforts to change Robbie seemed to her – to Jane, that is – derisory and worthy of the kind of mockery the Denny bitch was obviously purveying.

– That's it, she thought. I'm finished with this place.

The following evening, she was to go to Sarnia with Robbie. They had planned to see a production of *Oklahoma!*, the first play Robbie would see since a class trip to Stratford in Grade 12. Robbie was not keen, but she was looking forward to it and it suddenly occurred to her that she wanted to see the play with someone who could appreciate it. So, she went with William Marshall instead. William, who was not interested in women the way 'normal' men are interested in women, was the man you went out with when you couldn't stand the company of men. This worked well for everyone. For the women, it was wonderful to be out with a man who had good taste. For the men, it was sheer relief to know there was at least one man in town (the sacrificial lamb) who would go to the theatre or the ballet or the opera with their wives or girlfriends but who was no threat to womankind.

(How William himself felt about this, no one had the least interest. It was understood that Marshall was a man who loved men, but life was too short to think about such things unless you absolutely had to.)

Robbie was annoyed. That is, he was relieved to have escaped the theatre, but Jane had not told him what she was up to. He'd called at her parents' house at the appointed hour and had been told Jane had already left. That was it. He knew he had to be careful about what he said to her, but there had to be, if not respect between them, then at least consideration. He could, he thought, have been forgiven for wondering if she truly loved him.

Two days later, while they were at Jane's watching television, Robbie ventured a cautious

– I think you should have told me you were going to the play with Marshall.

Just the opening she had hoped for.

– It was none of your business.

– How was it none of my business when we were supposed to be going together and you didn't tell me?

– I don't have to tell you everything I do.

– Well, I can see you don't want to talk about this.

– You don't know *what* I want to talk about, you stupid hick.

– Why am I stupid?

Thus ended the polite part of the conversation. From here, things turned feral. Anything Jane could use against him, she used against him: his lack of culture, his insensitivity to her needs, the clumsy way he touched her, the way he took her for granted. Worst of all, she dug into him for the way he had treated Elizabeth Denny. He had betrayed Elizabeth, she said. He was a conniving son of a bitch who didn't care for anyone but himself. In fact, given the way he'd treated his fiancée, he was bound to betray her too, because he was selfish, stupid, mean, rotten, a prick and – for good measure – a jerk.

Some of what she accused him of being was, to some extent, true. He *had* been selfish, mean and stupid lately. But at least at the beginning of her attack, Jane did not really believe Robbie was as bad as all that. Her words were said as if with a crooked smile. As the catalogue of his sins grew, however, so did her conviction that he was despicable. (For one thing, it was impressive how many insults did apply to him. It felt as if she could have called him anything short of murderer and meant it.) In the space of half an hour, she had worked herself into a real hatred for Robbie, which became entangled in her hatred for Barrow.

However, Jane's attack was so unexpected and brutal it overshot its mark. Robbie was not put off or offended. He imagined it was her 'time of the month' and, as usual, he didn't know how to react. Should he laugh, show affection, comfort her, speak French? He opted to speak French *and* try to comfort her. This was the worst choice possible, in part because Jane was in no mood to be comforted, in even larger part because the only French he knew was 'Voulez-vous coucher avec moi?,' a phrase he inevitably mangled.

During a break in what was becoming Jane's screed, a break she took for breath and to think up some more effective line of attack, Robbie smiled timidly and said

— *Vous voulez coucher avec toi?*

He then put his hand on her thigh and moved as if to sidle up beside her and give her a hug. It was as if she had been bitten by a snake. She jumped up from the chesterfield on which they were sitting and cried out

— Don't touch me!

Robbie stood up, palms out, and apologized, confused that his effort to give comfort had gone so far astray. But the very look of him was a provocation to her. She had (she was convinced) only ever felt anything for him because his body was all muscle and perfect. (The words 'first love' didn't occur to her at this moment.) Now that the sight of him disgusted her, what was left but resentment of her own lust?

Though she was an articulate woman, none of her thoughts made it into words. What came out was a cry of frustration, and she attacked him, hitting him with her small fists, kicking him where she could, though what she wanted was to crush his testicles flat. She might have succeeded too. It was difficult for Robbie to protect himself against the onslaught of both feet and fists. Luckily for him, though, the sound of Jane's cries, of his repeated apologies, of flesh hitting flesh, brought Jane's parents into the room.

Seeing that the assault was one-sided, Mr. Richardson restrained his daughter as best he could, folding his arms around her from behind and lifting her up, then, with surprising calm, advising Robbie that it was perhaps time he left. He said

— I don't know how long I can hold her, son

as if he were restraining a panther.

Hobbling, Robbie escaped from the Richardsons', falling into the evening rain and the safety of his truck. He had never been so grateful to leave a woman. What a mistake he'd made. What a terrible mistake. He should never have had anything to do with Jane Richardson when he'd had the true love of a woman like Liz. He'd been betrayed by his feelings. As he drove home, he imagined he had learned a valuable lesson. But what lesson was there? He had fallen in love with Jane. What could one do about that? Nevertheless, he repented as he fled, the lights of the truck bounding over the dirt road like white horses.

The following day, Jane Richardson felt as if a door out of Barrow had finally opened. She'd wanted to leave for some time, of course, but had been held back by what now seemed like insignificant things: nostalgia, first love, fear of homesickness. None of that mattered anymore. As if all she owned had been lost in a fire, she was bereft but free, free to do what she wanted, free to rebuild from nothing. There was, maybe, a small twinge where Robbie was concerned, but this was something she could deal with.

She knew she was leaving, knew for sure it was a matter of days, not months, there being so little to take with her. As if to test her freedom, she walked around Barrow trying to imagine what she would miss, defying the town to make her stay. A light rain was falling. The world was slick and gleamed by shrouded sunlight. The town smelled of damp earth and damp concrete and the flowers in the park, lightly battered by rainfall, gave up their various perfumes. Here and there, the bitter smell of weeds dominated. Cars and pickups passed, *shush*ing as they went.

This bucolic mirage inspired nothing in her but boredom. She wanted no part of the flowers or the distantly grumbling thunder or the familiar smells that issued from the shops along Main Street. Coming up to Harrington's Bakery, no longer intimidated because she was no longer concerned with Barrow, she decided to go in. Elizabeth Denny was there, of course, and was not pleased to see her.

Mr. Harrington and the customers in the shop acted as if everything were fine, though all knew something was up. After a moment, Elizabeth excused herself from work and accompanied Jane outside. They stood under the bakery's awning, out of the rain.

— What do you want? asked Elizabeth. You come to gloat?

— No, said Jane. I came to apologize.

— Why would that be?

— Because I made a mistake I'm sorry about.

— You mean sleeping with my fiancé?

— I mean having anything to do with him. It was wrong. I don't love him.

— It's a little late to tell me that.

— I know and I'm sorry about that too. You don't always know things when it counts. I'm sure you've realized things a little late.

— No, said Elizabeth.

— You're a better person than me, then. Anyways, I wish things could be different between us, but I'm leaving Barrow. You won't ever have to see my face again.

— That's what you came to say?

— Yes.

— Well, I don't really care what you do or where you go. My relationship with Robbie's over, thanks to you. So, I can't wish you well. I think you're a cow, to tell the truth, but I'm glad you're going. Have a nice life.

— I'm sorry you see things that way, said Jane, but I wanted you to know I was sorry.

These were the last words she spoke to Elizabeth Denny. In fact, this was the last time she saw her. Elizabeth turned away, went back into the bakery and closed the door behind her. From the moment they parted, Jane was, more or less, done with Barrow. She told her parents she'd had enough. She told her friends she was going to New York – although she actually ended up in Toronto – and she was gone.

A long time coming yet suddenly upon her, her last impression of the land that had given birth to her was vague. The clouds were black and there was thunder. Even in her Greyhound cocoon, Jane felt as if she were being grumbled at. It was dark as the bus pulled away from the post office – her bewildered parents there to watch her go – so she saw very little. Rain the colour of husked rice was as if flung against the bus windows, blurring her vision of the land she knew best.

Of course, she did not escape Barrow entirely. There is not world enough to escape from home. Over the years, what she had thought of as the steely grip of the land loosened and became a light touch until, at times, as she walked along the lakeshore from Springhurst Avenue, where she lived, she would feel Barrow at her elbow, a discreet presence: wordless, soundless, ghostly but there; Barrow, like her own Eurydice, unfading as long as she did not look back, gone when she tried to remember this or that detail.

Though Robbie did not think so, Jane had done him a favour. She had burned the bridges between them once and for all. Also, she had left and he was not going to go to New York – her rumoured destination – to win her back. So, the only thing for him to do was suffer.

He did not suffer as one might have thought he would, though. Yes, he loved Jane and he would continue to do so for the rest of his life, whenever he thought of her. But he did not think of her often. His was not the kind of mind that nursed resentment and hurt. Jane had left him and given him a bloody lip for a souvenir. When the lip was back to its usual state, Jane had gone and she became a sporadic memory. The problem now was Liz. He saw her almost every day. His love had no chance to dissipate. And although it was unusual for him, he began to contemplate his behaviour. Had he, perhaps, done wrong despite doing things for love? Was love not the highest virtue and good?

None of his friends – that is, the Biglands, mostly – thought less of him. None of them could see that he'd done anything wrong. When they spoke of his situation at all, the general feeling was that loving two women at once might be a nuisance, but if so it was a nuisance compensated by variety.

One snippet of conversation went like this:

— A man could be real happy, someone said, if he had two women. You don't hear any bulls complaining and they've got to service way more than two cows.

— Yeah, but a bull doesn't love a cow. It's not the same.

— No one knows that for sure. Bulls get jealous, don't they?

— And no one can say if a man loves a woman for sure, either, 'cept for the man.

— If *he* even knows. I'm not sure I've ever been in love, even if I felt like I was now and then.

— I know I haven't and I don't want to be.

The friends were talking in the kitchen. From the living room, Mr. Bigland called out

— What the hell's wrong with you pantywaists. That's enough talking about love! You boys are embarrassing your mother.

Those words had ended all talk about feelings, but parts of the conversation recurred to Robbie as he went about his life. Was it possible that there was no such thing as love? He tried to think that way, but he could not. It made no sense, because although there were any number of women who could get his engine working, there had only ever been two who could touch something deeper in him. There had only ever been two women he would surrender his happiness to please. It was far from certain there would ever be another. And what would it be like to live a life endlessly fucking but feeling nothing deeper than that an itch had been scratched? He did not care to know. It didn't matter to him what you called it, but as far as he was concerned he loved Liz Denny and he would not give up trying to make her see that he did, that he always would and that it hurt him to be without her. Not for a moment did it occur to him that his love might not have the significance for Elizabeth that it had for him. The only question Robbie entertained was how to speak what was inside him in such a way that Liz would see past his mistakes (such as they had been) and past his flaws (such as they were) to the solid emotion within him.

He simply had to speak to her again.

He chose a Saturday, a month or so after Jane had gone. He waited for Liz as she left Harrington's. She had a ride. She didn't need him, but he asked anyway if he could take her home ('No') or if she would meet him at their clearing behind her uncle's farm.

– Why? she asked.

– You don't have to if you don't want to, but there's things I want to tell you.

Elizabeth thought about it. She thought

– *Well, it's not as if I wasn't ever going to speak to him again*

and said

– Okay

though it had just rained and the ground would be impassable in places.

– I don't want to hear anything about how much you love me, she added.

The woods had already begun to change colour. Some of the leaves had turned yellow and orange, and the pine trees, encouraged by the rain, spread their scent as if they were in mating season. The ground was muddy in spots. The only practical thing to wear were wellingtons and, of course, stepping in the wrong place made it feel as if your boots wanted to stay behind.

Robbie arrived before Elizabeth. It was not yet dark but he'd brought a flashlight, just in case they talked until darkness. Not that either of them needed light to find their way home, but it occurred to him that it might be gentlemanly to have a flashlight to offer, on the off chance she wanted one.

Elizabeth, when she arrived, was all business.

– What do you want? she asked.

– I just …

he said, suddenly self-conscious.

– I just wanted to say …

he said, unwilling to say much, for fear it be the wrong thing.

– I just wanted to tell you how much I miss you.

– It's always about you, she said, about how much you love me, how much you miss me. Have you thought for a second about how I feel?

Risking everything, he answered honestly.

– No, he said, I haven't.

– Why not?

– I'm a little ... I'm not smart like you are, Lizzie. I try to think about others, but I don't always manage to in time. But I do think about you and how you make me feel. I haven't always done the right thing. I'm sorry.

He meant it and she knew he meant it. After all, knowing someone well means knowing all the signs of genuine emotion, and they had known each other since they were children. She knew that he was struggling to say what she already knew, struggling to say it with the right words, though so little of what anything means comes through words. Here he was, wishing for an eloquence his body and spirit already possessed. What good would it have done for him to go on like some lost troubadour? What was that poem they'd studied in Grade 12?

> *When I see leaves, flowers and pears*
> *appearing on the branches and hear*
> *the birds in the woods sing,*
> *then Love buds, blooms and bears fruit in me ...*

Devil-tongued bastards, all of them. Anyway, she already knew that he loved her, missed her and wanted her back. What she didn't know was if any of that counted.

– You're sorry, she said. What does that change?

–I don't know, Lizzie, but it should change something, shouldn't it?

– Yes, she said, I guess it's nice to know you're sorry.

– I'm not saying you have to or anything, but I'd still like to ...

– You want me to marry you, after what you put me through?

– I'm not saying you have to or anything. I'm just saying maybe think about it if you still love me, 'cause none of this is ever going to happen again. I swear it on the Bible.

How little he knew himself. If it was true that he hadn't sought to be in love with two women at once, how could he possibly know if it would or would not happen again? And now she had a perfectly good idea how he would behave if it did. The next time, however, the next time, if she married him, there might be children involved. Would that stop him? Or was it *amor vincit omnia* forever and ever? There was no telling, from this side of the divide, just what he might do.

– What if it does happen again? she asked.

– It won't, he answered. Lightning doesn't strike the same place twice.

Again his lack of self-knowledge was flagrant. But how little he knew her! It was bad enough that he'd not known how hurt she would be by this Jane Richardson business, but he rarely knew how to reassure her when she needed it most. He had known her for as long as she had known him. How could he not know her feelings?

– What do you think I'm feeling now? she asked.

– I think you're feeling like I don't know what you're feeling, he answered.

She looked at him – his brown hair pasted to his forehead, his eyes looking into hers – and saw that his attention was entirely given to her, as it rarely was except when they were making love. It occurred to her that he did know her somewhat and that at times he did have the right answer. These were thoughts that, despite herself, gave her pleasure.

Well, after all, it took time to fall out of love. She was vulnerable and knew it.

– I've got to go home, she said.

– You want me to come with you? I brought a flashlight.

– No, I don't want you to walk me home. I'll call you.

In the end, if you could call it winning, she had, she supposed, won. She had Robbie to herself, if she wanted him.

She should have been ... if not pleased, then at least satisfied. But it was not so simple. What was there to feel satisfied about, really? She had learned a lesson about her fiancé and it had marred her picture of him. Also, the idea that she had 'won' him from Jane Richardson was repulsive. And again: by now, it seemed everyone between Barrow and Sarnia knew her business. One day, she'd gone to Petrolia to see Dr. Reidl and even there it seemed people knew all about her situation. The way they looked at her with sympathy. Christ on a cross! Nowadays, everyone had sympathy for her, and the more sympathy they had the worse it was. She couldn't give change without feeling the weight of an unstated 'you poor girl.' Hard to find satisfaction in any of that.

Then there was *the* question. Did she still want Robbie? Not did she still love him. She did, she supposed, if only out of long-standing habit. But that did not mean she would do anything for him. So, did she want to marry the man? The answer was yes and no. It had been yes and no for some time. She had not, for instance, cancelled the wedding. She'd meant to, but hadn't got round to it while her friends and family made ready for the happy day. Had she been hoping for Robbie to come back to her? Not that she was aware. Had she been hoping for another husband? No, not at all. Why then had she not been able to speak the handful of simple words: 'I can't marry him, after what he's put me through'?

Now, unexpectedly, it was a question of keeping the day of her wedding. She could, if she wanted, marry the man she'd been hoping to marry. Perhaps it really was significant that she hadn't called the wedding off. Perhaps it meant that, deep within, there had been (there was still) an undiminished hope that Robbie would return to her. Maybe the love she'd felt for him would survive its transplant to this new world in which she was not sure what she wanted.

It had been a rainy day, the rain falling slantwise against the stained glass of the church so that Alexis the beggar seemed to be begging underwater.

After a confession during which she'd told the priest everything (all her feelings, all that had happened between her and Robbie), Elizabeth and Father Pennant sat together at the front of the church.

– I think you're right, he said. Love isn't the only thing to consider. Love between a man and a woman is perishable because men and women are fallible. There is no perfect love, here below. You love him and he's shown that he loves you … in his way. You need to decide if that's enough, but, in my opinion, you're fortunate. You know the worst of him. You know his selfishness and his thought-lessness. You've had your eyes opened. If you can still love him, under the circumstances, that's a blessing. And then, too, maybe you've gone through the worst.

– You think so?

– I don't know for sure, he answered, because I don't know Robbie well. But I know you well enough to guess that you know the answer. I think you have a good idea if worse is to come. It's a matter of listening to yourself.

Thunder sounded and the rain renewed its onslaught on the saints. Hard to know one's own mind in the din.

– You've been helpful, Elizabeth said.

From that moment she tried to listen to her own feelings. Had she gone through the worst? Was Robbie capable of putting her through unendurable humiliation? Or was he, as he insisted, a man who had been 'prey to a love he couldn't fight off'? (Hearing those words made her wonder if he'd been reading, though, of course, he hadn't finished a book since they were in high school. The words had almost certainly been Jane's.) Were there other loves out there to prey on him? Could she endure those if she had to? 'Listening to herself' brought neither comfort nor certainty. What it brought were questions about herself, about her capacity to forgive, about her ability to imagine the worst and yet to go on in a way that would allow her the self-respect she needed to survive.

Her wedding was a month away. Elizabeth allowed herself this thought: if, on the morning of her wedding, she decided she could not live with Robbie Myers, she would say no at the altar. It would be a costly and cruel no, but she would say it, and the idea she *could* say no brought with it a yes. On the appointed day there would be a wedding. She could not say if there would be a marriage.

Father Pennant was not at peace with himself either.

To begin with, there was the situation with Lowther. He was no longer annoyed with Lowther. He was worried about him. Lowther had begun to accept that he was in perfect health and that the chances of his dying were slim, but acceptance had brought distance. Lowther executed his tasks and practised his cello, but he no longer followed Father Pennant around, preferring his own company and the comfort of lugubrious music – all of it for the cello, all of it sounding dirge-like.

Then there were his own feelings of anomie. It was taxing to sense one was not part of the community in which one found oneself. He went about his work, comforting the bereaved, marrying happy couples, visiting the sick and infirm. But he was himself in need of a comfort that did not come. What relief he took, he took from the fields around town, drawing pictures of the flora and fauna in his notebooks.

Sometime after speaking to Liz Denny about her marriage, he went for a walk that took him miles out of town to an abandoned farm. The farm had once belonged to George Preston, a farmer who had been well-loved by all in Barrow. Preston had died a year before Father Pennant's arrival and in that time the farm had been untended, waiting for a buyer, its apple trees and rows of strawberries growing wild. Behind the orchard and the field of strawberries, there was a wooded area through which a shallow creek ran. Father Pennant made for the creek, looking for toads, fish, moss, reeds and cattails.

It had rained only hours before he set off, so the land smelled of greenery and muck. The congeries of smells was intoxicating. How many things he could distinguish by their scent! There was everything from the wet earth itself to the trunks of fallen trees with their tenacious mushrooms, from the sweet smell of rotting apples to the slightly sour odour of the creek bed. And all of it brought solace.

He had followed the creek for a while when he heard bells and bleating and saw, on the opposite side of the creek, four sheep: a group of three following behind one that did not have a bell and did not bleat. Beautiful creatures: dark-legged, dark-faced, their white fleeces recently shorn, their ears twitching as a cloud of midges pestered them. He was about to move on when, in an odd instant, he had the distinct impression that the lead sheep had spotted him and wished to approach. The sheep stepped into the creek and, almost daintily, forded the shallow stream. It was unnerving to watch.

Father Pennant stood still where he was. The sheep, once it had crossed, shook itself the way dogs do, and a frisson travelled back and forth along its whitish flank. The sheep then approached, until it was a yard or so before him.

– Walk with me, Christopher, said the sheep.

It then turned away and followed the bank of the creek, taking the path Father Pennant himself might have. This, thought Father Pennant, was an excellent illusion, better than the gypsy moths had been and better by far than the ridiculous walk on water the mayor had taken. Having been prepared for the unusual by the previous 'miracles,' he was amused, not at all awed or frightened by the sheep. He looked for a speaker or microphone where, no doubt, the bell collar should have been. Was the sheep even real, he wondered, and found himself admiring all the work that must have gone into the illusion.

– Who are you? asked Father Pennant.

– I am He who has no one name, said the sheep.

– Are you? asked Father Pennant. You must prefer one over the others.

The sheep stopped where it was and looked across the creek at the place it had been.

– No, it said. I like them all.

Very clever, thought Father Pennant, recognizing or seeming to recognize both the wit and the voice of Lowther Williams. How wonderful to have Lowther back to his old playful self.

– Don't you believe in me? asked the sheep.

– I believe, said Father Pennant, in God the Father and Christ His Son and I believe in the Holy Ghost. What I don't believe in is talking sheep.

Stopping again to stare across the suddenly noiseless creek, the sheep said

– Christopher, how do you know that I am not your Lord?

– My Lord has no reason to speak to me, he answered. I'm not the kind of man God seeks out. You have me confused with some other, better man.

– Lowther has broken your faith, said the sheep.

Father Pennant smiled. His spirits lifted and he entered more fully into the game. He spoke to the sheep – Lowther, obviously – as if it were, in fact, God.

– There is something you can do for me, he said. Teach me to be satisfied with the world and everything that's in it.

– My son, said the sheep, that's a tragic thing you're asking me to give. You should not be satisfied with the things of this world, however seductive they are.

Father Pennant laughed.

– No, he said, that is exactly what I want. No miracles, just the plants and animals and the sky above. That's all the mystery I need.

– I'll give you what you've asked for, said the sheep, but allow me a few words. You're on a road that leads to disappointment. Of course, it's wonderful to contemplate Nature, but without the miraculous the earth is only a coffin. What you should ask for is a restoration of your belief in miracles. You would still have the earth and all that's beautiful, but you would again be open to more than you can conceive. Let me help you imagine it. Look over there. I will set those trees on fire.

No sooner said than three maple trees on the other side of the creek caught fire: flames from their roots to their highest leaves. It

132

was a peculiar fire, though: noiseless and without smoke. The flames themselves were more like supple red and orange crystal. It was like the idea of fire rather than fire itself. A hologram, thought Father Pennant, one of Heath's holograms. But it was impressive all the same.

– That's lovely, said Father Pennant. Well done. Really well done, but I prefer the trees to the illusion.

– I understand, said the sheep, and I'll give you what you've asked for. From now on you will be satisfied by the things of the earth. If ever, someday, you wonder if there is more, come back to this place and cut those three trees. The first will bleed, the second will give honey and from the third you'll have water. If ever you do this, you will know that I am the Lord and that there is more to the world than the world itself.

– It's a deal, said Father Pennant, smiling.

He turned toward the maples. They were no longer alight. He turned back to admire the sheep, but it had gone. The hologram, it seemed, had been turned off. A perfect illusion. And it was a joy to have had things done so well. He supposed that Heath and Lowther had prepared the trees so they would bleed, give honey or water. He was tempted to try them, so their time and effort would not be wasted, but he was tired. He had been walking for a while and it was time to go back. Moreover, he was impatient to talk to Lowther, to tell him how much he appreciated all the work they'd done in order to test him. His spirits were raised. He was deeply moved by the care that had gone into the illusion. He saw the attention to detail – the sheep, the trees on fire – as a form of respect, and he was grateful to Lowther.

The thought that he had actually encountered God was amusing, but it did not stay with him for long. He did not believe that any supreme being would waste its time on him and, perhaps more significantly, he did not want the attention of God. The miraculous was the last thing he wanted. And if he avoided testing the trees for blood, honey and water, it was not only from fatigue. It was also because, deep inside, he refused to entertain the idea that the sheep he'd seen was divine.

As he walked along the road home, his thoughts turned to Elizabeth Denny. He wondered if Lowther could come up with an illusion that would amaze her and direct her thoughts to the things she needed to take into account: Nature above all. It struck him, in fact, that the same sheep he'd seen might well work for Elizabeth, because he took, as he walked back to the rectory, such joy in the natural world: the sharp pine smell of the spruce trees, the wet earth drying in late afternoon sunlight, the stillness of the clouds above. In other words, it couldn't hurt to have Elizabeth feel how great the world was, how sufficient. It was a feeling that put everything else into perspective.

V

AS AUTUMN COMES

As Father Pennant was thinking about Elizabeth and the peace
Nature might bring her, Elizabeth was thinking – again and
again and inescapably – about love. She wondered what, exactly,
love was and if she was, in fact, possessed by it. Like a cloud of
midges, the questions pestered her.

Why did people *fall* in love? Why *in* love? Wasn't love within
us? Was the love within different from the love one fell into? Did
love need an object? Did it need a person? Was love still love if unre-
quited? Was it love if the object of one's love was unworthy? Could
she marry a man she no longer loved in the hope she would fall in
love with him again?

Any *one* of these questions could have kept a mind busy for
months. Worse, all of them had answers that were as difficult to deal
with as the questions themselves. The answers seemed to lead her
further and further from her own feelings. In any case, they did not
bring her closer to Robbie. Nor did they make her decision to carry
through with the wedding easier to accept. Never had she been so

unsure of anything. In the past, when doubt or ambivalence troubled her, Elizabeth had turned to her work for comfort. Doing, doing *something*, was her best way out of the disquiet: learning to make bread, helping her aunt and uncle with whatever needed to be done – housecleaning or sod cutting. But her doubts about love could not be quelled by physical activity.

So, what *was* love to her? It was Robbie and it was not Robbie. It was Robbie's body, his arms and back. It was nothing physical, though it could be set off by the physical, by the memory of the physical, by the memory of a memory. Love was a scene in which she saw herself. It was at the heart of who she was. It was peripheral. It was a moment. It was a thousand moments she had shared with Robbie. But it did not matter that it was Robbie in particular because, in these moments, adrift from herself, she was not Elizabeth Denny. Love was a kind of anonymity, an anonymity in which she was (chiefly) 'a woman in love.' It turned her into someone else, into Charlotte Brontë, into Emma Bovary, into the woman in *Brief Encounter*, so in love with Trevor Howard she would sacrifice her happiness for him. No sooner did she imagine herself as other, however, than she was thrown back on the very Elizabethness of everything she was and all that she wanted. And so, at nearly every turn, waiting like a sentinel for the answer to the first question ('What is love?'), was a further question: 'Who am I?'

> *What is love/ Who am I?*
> *Who am I/ What is love?*

Neither question could be answered without answering the other.

Unexpectedly, this impasse brought relief. 'Who am I?' was a more daunting question, in some ways, than 'What is love?,' but thinking about herself and her life, her aspirations and desires, brought the question of love into sharper focus. It became clearer to Elizabeth that, whatever love was, she was no longer the girl who had been 'in love' with Robbie Myers. She was a woman considering marriage with a man named Robert Myers, a man she now knew as fallible, someone who was as liable to hurt her as not. It was a gift to know this, to think it, to face its implications.

As Elizabeth was thinking about love and Father Pennant was thinking about Nature, Lowther Williams was thinking about life.

Lowther had become ridiculous to himself. So, when weeks after his sixty-third birthday, his depression lifted, he was relieved. He began to see things in a more forgiving light. God had decided differently than he, Lowther, might have wished. Was that reason to behave like a spoiled child? Wasn't it more sensible to treat the leftover life he had been given as a gift? He would be the first male in his line to see sixty-four, if he kept up his health. And he resolved to keep up his health, though he also kept an eye on the possibility that God would, in His own way, take him before he saw sixty-four. No tragedy, that. He had already been given more time than his father.

Of course, he had not planned for a long life. He had to think about how this unanticipated portion might best be led. Should he now spend the money he had spent years saving (and which he had promised to Father Pennant)? What would he spend it on? He was a man who desired nothing. He had travelled all over the world. He had eaten wonderful food. He had read all the books he considered necessary – from Aristotle's *Metaphysics* to Zamyatin's *We* – in preparation for an early (or, rather, timely) death. His cello was not the best. There were certainly more expensive, warmer instruments than his, but he loved this cello, these pieces of wood that he had touched and held, daily, for so many years. Needing no cello, no exotic food, no new books, he could not think what he would do with money. So, there was the first decision made for him: he would continue his frugal existence.

Would he continue his work at the parish? Heath had asked Lowther to consider working with him, and the idea was appealing. Working for Heath, he would not be bored. But Lowther had had all the excitement he needed from life. The simplicity and quiet of the rectory was more appealing. So, he would stay with Father

Pennant. In fact, as he prepared to live out his last days (or months, or years), the only change of routine Lowther made was to take an hour in the evening to write music, a thing he had thought about doing for years.

On the day Father Pennant was accosted by the sheep, Lowther went to the Thames River with no purpose in mind. He sat on the grass by the bank of the river and watched the river run. The sun was warm, but not oppressive, after a rain. The ground was damp, but Lowther did not mind. He had a copy of the *Barrow Topic*, the town's newspaper, under him. The clouds above were white. There was a slight breeze that, from time to time, brought a whiff of rotting fish. Somewhere further along, a catfish or a carp or even a pike must have died and washed up on the banks of the Thames. Growing wild along the riverbank: goldenrods, thistles, clover, chicory and, of course, grass: grass that was green, sparse where people walked, grass that made it look as if a hillock beside the river had a bad comb-over.

The most beautiful aspect of the afternoon was the river. No, not the river, which included both water and bank, but rather the water itself. The water was various tints of green, blue or bluish green, with silvery-white eddies where it moved around the stones and clumps of reeds close to the shore. The water was like the tail of a long animal – something living and entirely unconcerned with the life beyond its unpredictably twisting bed. As Lowther watched, he was reminded of Tomasine Humble. Lowther hadn't liked her any more than most people had. She had been the very definition of miserable. But one summer afternoon, an afternoon much like this one, he had been out for a walk. It must have been a weekday, sometime before the end of school, because, at least in his memory, there had been no one else around. He had seen the old woman sitting alone, her back to the world, her feet in the water.

It was odd that his memory had taken so deep an impression of such an insignificant moment. Lowther experienced a rush of sympathy for the poor woman. It wasn't easy not knowing when death

138

would come. This ignorance now united them, though he was years younger than she had been on the day he'd seen her with her feet in the water.

Lowther took off his shoes and socks, walked to the side of the river, sat on a rock and allowed both of his feet to rest on a flat stone beneath the surface. His feet, as the clear water ran over them, were distorted, slightly distended, and looked as if they had been fixed to his ankles at an amusing angle. How wonderful life was!

He had been staring at the river for some time, moving his feet over the velvet grime of his underwater shelf, when the time came to return to the rectory to prepare an evening meal for Father Pennant. Lowther stood up, but too quickly. The blood rushed from his head and, disoriented, he stepped into the river where, landing barefoot onto a smooth stone, he slipped, falling over sideways, hitting his head on a rock, passing out and drowning in water not six inches deep. No final words, no last rites, no deep thoughts, no music. Just a quick incursion of darkness, a darkness that was itself like a river.

It would be difficult to exaggerate the sadness Father Pennant felt when he was asked to identify Lowther's body in the morgue. He had been called not long after the body entered the morgue, so that, when the sheet was lifted to show Lowther's face, Lowther's hair was still damp. It had not been combed back. It clung to his forehead and right cheek. At his left temple, there was dried mud, and that was the most disturbing detail. It was so unlike Lowther to look dishevelled, as if he had been in a fight of some sort. His corpse looked almost exactly like him, but not quite. And Father Pennant felt as if this whole business were another of Lowther's tests to see his reaction. It was hard to keep himself from gently slapping Lowther's face and telling him, 'Stop, now. That's enough. This is disturbing, Lowther. Please get up.'

– Is everything all right, Father? asked the attendant.

– Yes, he answered. I'm fine. Thank you.

He walked out of the morgue, dazed.

There were two facets of Lowther's death that Christopher Pennant found difficult to take in. First, there was the sheer fact of Lowther's being gone. It was impossible for him to reconcile the fallen trunk of flesh with the living being it had once been. It was almost easier to believe that the man had gone to Europe, say, and left his body behind for when he returned. Of course, this was how he always felt about the dead. None of them stayed and yet it was as if none of them had gone. It wasn't the finality of death that surprised him. It was the ghostly persistence of life. As if to say, it isn't the dead who haunt the living; it's the living who haunt the dead.

Even more difficult to encompass: Lowther had died, as he said he would, at the age of sixty-three. Father Pennant had not, until the very moment he looked down at Lowther's grey face, believed him. The idea that God would kill on schedule was ludicrous. It was like those at Medjugorje who had regular appointments with the Virgin: not only absurd but petty, if true. One had to imagine the Lord keeping an eye on His datebook. But could you really call Lowther's death accidental? It was a disturbingly precise accident, if so. Which was it then? Accident or divine intervention? In the days immediately following Lowther's death, Father Pennant chose 'accident' and let it go at that. There was too much to do: a eulogy to write, Lowther's things to dispose of or to put in order, arrangements to be made.

Hours after seeing Lowther's body in the morgue, Father Pennant tried to write a eulogy for Lowther's funeral. His first effort was filled with platitudes. Lowther had gone 'to a better place,' 'God had called Lowther to Him,' Lowther's memory would be 'evergreen' for those who had known him. Reading his own words back, he felt as if he had betrayed someone. He rewrote everything. He wrote the eulogy three or four times, from 'Please be seated' to 'Amen.' He then rewrote it a few more times before it became clear that he had no idea what he thought about Lowther's death. He had feelings, but they weren't yet settled in him. Was it really good that God should call the 'traveller' home? Was death a better place, a reward that waited? Was it loving of God to have made us for death and, if so, why should

God's love need explaining? Was there any love worthy of the name that could be explained?

Days passed and not one of the words he had written, save 'Amen,' remained unchanged or unexamined. He thought fleetingly, but more than once, of allowing someone else to write the sermon for him. That seemed worse than mouthing clichés, though. It seemed cowardly.

The problem was that he had, in some measure, succumbed to the sheep's curse. He actually did find it more difficult now than he had previously to imagine a world 'beyond,' a world beyond this beautiful world. How prescient the sheep (that is, Lowther or one of his friends) had been to suggest that greater sensitivity to this world meant a weakening of the hold God had on the imagination. In the midst of his rewrites, Father Pennant began to think of death as nothing but an end, and how was one to speak of a cul-de-sac or a bricked-up exit? Death was no more than the termination of lively functions, the collective refusal to go on of a group of organs that had, moments before, collectively refused to desist. It was an end, no more to be mourned or explained than the end of a symphony, the final pages of a book, the last daub of paint applied to a canvas. And so, death: significant only in being the last of something. But if death had so little significance, what did that make of life? Wasn't life, as they say, given its poignancy and meaning by death?

Yes, finally a cliché that he could use. Death gave poignancy to life. It was the shadow in Arcadia. A field through which a river ran, white clouds, wheat in stooks – all was made more precious by the presence of evening: a touch of crimson, deepening shadows, the time of day when it was not possible to tell dog from wolf. Lowther had lived a long twilight. From the moment his father had told him that he, Lowther, would die at sixty-three, Lowther had lived in anticipation of night, and now night had come. It was not to be mourned. Certainly, the passing of Lowther's spirit was sad for those who had loved him. But death was nothing and there was nothing beyond it that was of concern for those who remained.

In the eulogy he delivered, Father Pennant did not (of course) say that there was 'nothing in death that is of concern for the living.' He shared his thoughts about Arcadia before going on to recall his most precious memory of Lowther, a man he had not known for long – five months, was it? – but whom he had come to treasure. For at least two weeks, Lowther had been baking bread, dozens and dozens of loaves. At times, every surface in the kitchen had been whitened by flour. Lowther had thrown out many of the loaves he'd made. Others, they had eaten. These had been wonderful, but Lowther had been unsatisfied with them. Father Pennant did not understand Lowther's sudden passion for bread until, one evening, as they sat down for supper, Lowther brought out a loaf that tasted familiar and smelled of yeast, molasses and burnt walnuts. In order to apologize for his bad mood in the days after he'd failed to die, Lowther had perfectly duplicated Harrington's brown bread, Father Pennant's favourite. And Lowther, having gotten the recipe right, had baked a further dozen of the loaves. There were eleven of them still in the rectory's freezer, and Christopher Pennant did not know if it were best to eat them or to preserve them in Lowther's memory.

Lowther's funeral came quickly and went quickly by. Because Lowther had kept to himself for the most part, the funeral was not well-attended. Heath was there, of course, as were a handful of people from Sarnia and a man from Petrolia whose name was Tully. There were some ten people in all, if you included the altar boys.

The day was sunny, so the stained-glass images were brightly lit. The saints, Zeno and Zenobius, went about their business, laughing or raising the dead, in what looked like jewelled surroundings. The saints on the other side were in darker, but still striking, tones. There was a cheerfulness to the funeral, though Father Pennant was distraught at Lowther's death. At times during the mass, a wind blew through the church, carrying the smell of freshly cut grass.

Despite his efforts to think about his friend and to maintain seriousness, Father Pennant found his mood lightened as the service progressed so that, by the time he rose to give the eulogy, it was as if Lowther were there with him, and it would have been embarrassing to say too much or, worse, to be pompous. As a consequence, Father Pennant gave a moving eulogy, one that was pleasing to those who had known Lowther well.

At the cemetery, Father Pennant spoke a few warm words, commended Lowther's spirit to the care of the God Lowther had so fervently believed in. He and the others then left the place where, spiritually speaking, there was no trace of Lowther Williams.

Father Pennant was exhausted after the funeral. He was emotionally drained. However, he'd invited Heath Lambert to dinner and so, that evening, he had to tidy the rectory and prepare a meal for two: grilled pork, mashed fingerlings with green onions, and black pudding. It was all prepared as Lowther might have, but Father Pennant used a cookbook from England and a calculator to convert the weights and volumes.

The two men ate at seven o'clock. The setting sun was reddish but the spirit of the day had not dissipated. They spoke of Lowther. Though Heath had known him much longer than Father Pennant had, there were details of Lowther's life to which he had not been privy, details Lowther had confessed to the priest but that Father Pennant was loath to share.

Happy to talk about his truest friend, Heath wondered whether he or Father Pennant had known Lowther best. Clearly, Father Pennant knew more of the facts or, at least, Lowther's angle on the facts. But a man is more than the incidents that make up his life and more than what he judges significant or worth hiding. Heath Lambert felt that, were Lowther with them, he could predict Lowther's behaviour. And this, as Father Pennant himself admitted, was beyond the priest. Though they had been close over the months they'd lived together, Father Pennant had never – or never with any certainty – been able to say what his friend would do. Moreover, he still had a number of questions about Lowther. One of them concerned the sheep. After describing his encounter at Preston's farm to Heath, Father Pennant asked

– How did Lowther make the sheep talk?

– I don't know that he did, answered Heath. I don't know that he had anything to do with it. After you saw Mayor Fox walk on water, Lowther felt pretty guilty. He thought it was his fault you got such a shock. I don't think he wanted to put you through that again. He'd be the one to do it, I guess, if he changed his mind. I don't know how, though.

– A hologram, maybe?

– No, he'd have needed my help for that. And let me tell you: that was a costly business. Those gypsy moths were an expensive gift, if you know what I mean. And it took a lot of work.

– I was upset when he told me the moths were an illusion, said Father Pennant. I kind of knew before he confessed, but being sure was still a bit . . . unpleasant. It doesn't make you feel good to be fooled.

– I'm with you there, said Heath. I'd have been pissed too. But it was one hell of a thing to pull off. Felt like solving an equation.

– I thought the whole thing was diabolical, said Father Pennant.

– Diabolical? said Heath. I could get used to being lord of the moths. They'd make good wallpaper.

Both of them laughed.

Father Pennant had put out a small white plate filled with olive oil: a white circle that held a yellowish circle. Beside the plate of oil there was another plate on which there were rough slices of the bread Lowther had made. Heath took a piece of bread, dipped it in the olive oil, shook a few grains of salt over it and ate.

– Well, Father Pennant said, Lowther must have done the sheep thing somehow. Sheep don't go around talking.

– It would be good if they did, said Heath. Human conversation isn't always entertaining. You'd want to talk to the really smart sheep, though, the ones who'd thought about things.

– I don't know about that, said Father Pennant. The best thing about sheep is there's probably no sheep philosophy.

– That you know of, said Heath.

There really was something impish about Heath Lambert. He

was good company and Father Pennant could see why Lowther, a believer, had been close to Heath, the atheist. Of course, atheists were themselves believers and, inevitably, ended up on the same God-driven sledge as the faithful: He is, He is not, He is, He is not, ad infinitum. It was no surprise at all that Heath and Lowther had been close, when you thought about it.

— You knew Lowther's mind better than I did, said Father Pennant. Let's say he did make that sheep on Preston's farm. What was he trying to tell me with all that talk about Nature?

— You got me there, said Heath. I don't know. He was someone who really loved the earth. Every little detail about it. Mushrooms, insects, lice … there wasn't anything Lowther didn't love, but he managed to love God too. I don't think there was any difference between God and Nature, in his mind. Then again, maybe he really did think Nature isn't enough and he was trying to warn you, for some reason. Of course, if Lowther didn't have anything to do with this sheep, maybe you did see God. That'd be had luck, as far as I'm concerned. You look in the Bible. Once God speaks to you, your life's pretty much ruined, isn't it? Not too many happy prophets, are there, Father?

— No, said Father Pennant, that's true. Thank you for your thoughts, Heath. Most of what you said sounds exactly like Lowther's thinking. There's one more thing I'd like to ask. Lowther left me to take care of his money. What do you think he would have wanted me to do with it?

— I think he wanted you to do whatever you thought was best. He told me so. He trusted you, even if you only knew each other for a little while. He trusted you more than he trusted me, I can tell you. He thought I'd waste the money on the greenhouse I'm building. And he was right. I would spend it on my greenhouse. But you should do what you think is right.

— You mean give it to charity?

— If that's what you think is right. About the only thing we know for certain is that he didn't want to put his money in a greenhouse. If he had, he'd have left it for me.

The day was done. The sun torched the last of the clouds. An evening breeze blew through the rectory, playing with the tablecloth and the cloth napkins.

– That was a great meal, said Heath, rising.

– I'm glad you liked it, said Father Pennant. You should come around more often. I enjoy talking about Lowther.

– Listen, Father, said Heath, before I go I want to say something and I don't want you to take it the wrong way. I used to say this to Lowther all the time. I really don't know why someone as sharp as you would believe all that mumbo-jumbo the Church tells you. Even if you leave aside the whole question of God, there's no reason someone like you has to live on his knees, if you know what I mean. Don't get me wrong. I'm not the kind of atheist who hates people who don't believe what he does. I just wanted you to know how I feel, since we're likely to spend some time together and I don't want to hide anything.

– So you think the earth is enough?

– No, I don't. I think there's plenty we don't understand, plenty, and if the earth was enough we wouldn't have to go looking for it. What I think is: there's enough mystery in this life without dragging incense and holy trinities into it.

– I know what you mean, said Father Pennant, but I'm beginning to wonder if there's any real mystery or if the mystery's all in our heads. Maybe the earth *is* enough, Heath. Anyway, if I were going to lose my faith in God, I wouldn't replace it with faith in chance and nothingness.

Heath laughed and shook his finger as if to say no.

– That's exactly the kind of thing Lowther would have said. We're going to have to keep this conversation going.

The men shook hands and Heath walked from the rectory.

Though he lived outside of Barrow and he was, more or less, an atheist, Heath and Christopher Pennant would become close friends during the priest's short stay in Barrow. This was in part because each was bound in the other's memory with memories of Lowther, and they would inevitably speak of Lowther when they met. But it was also because they were – as they discovered – temperamentally suited and had a number of interests in common.

The weeks following Lowther's funeral were among the last that preceded Elizabeth's marriage to Robbie Myers. September 30th approached like the date of a final verdict.

A week before the wedding, members of her extended family began to arrive in Barrow. Her aunts, uncles, cousins and grandparents all came to wish her the best. The house she had lived in for most of her life, the house she would be leaving if she married Robbie, became a noisy and convivial world of Dennys, Youngs and Constables. It was a diverse but, at least over the short term, pleasant gathering of people. There were those who could not eat cheese and those on diets who ate nothing but fruit. There were those who would not sleep in soft beds and those who would sleep anytime and anywhere. There were any number of odd personalities and quirks of behaviour so that, at times, one wondered what it was that linked them all. But then, as if in answer to that very question, one noticed that most shared some physical feature or other: a nose, hazel-green eyes, ears that stuck out, body types. Depending on how one looked at it, 'family' was a word for a funhouse mirror in which Youngs, Dennys and Constables were changed and distorted or it was a word for what persisted despite the distortions. It was also, of course, a thing that held an intimation of her parents. As such, there was nothing more precious to her.

Along with the influx of family came Elizabeth's closest friends. They organized her bridal shower. They forced her to her own hen party, which was held on Ladies' Night at a strip club in Sarnia. The men were all nicely built, but the last thing Elizabeth wanted to do was to touch any man's package for luck. Her friends, who had set it up so Elizabeth could feel Donny the Horse for herself, were disappointed when she refused – this after they'd plied her with vodka and tonic. But they themselves manhandled the unfortunate Donny until Elizabeth felt sorry for him and wondered if a penis could bruise, a consideration that made her think of apples and, because the man was monstrously endowed, the arm of a shaken baby.

Throughout the week, Barrow itself seemed charged with a new spirit. On its streets, Elizabeth was warmly greeted by all those planning to attend the wedding. John Harrington made a seven-tiered wedding cake and, the day before the wedding, displayed it in the window of the bakery. Elizabeth herself was said to be radiant. Radiant, radiant, radiant, until she wondered if her skin tone had changed. Whenever she spoke to Robbie, he seemed resolute and happy, the very things she would have liked to be.

Then, because it was inevitable, her wedding day came. Elizabeth was awakened at five in the morning by her aunt Anne, who could not sleep. Her wedding day was, for her aunt and uncle, as so many Christmases had been for her. As the rest of the house slept, the three of them ate a simple breakfast – fresh milk, bran flakes and maple syrup – and then went out to the fields, their family alone together one final time. The sun, when it crested the horizon was so bright they turned to keep it at their backs, walking some distance without speaking. Elizabeth had nothing to say. Her uncle John, a quiet man anyway, could think of nothing to say. And her aunt Anne was overcome by emotion, and so no words came to her. After a while, John Young took his wife's arm and sang as they walked:

> Down the dusty road together
> Homeward pass the hurrying sheep
> Stupid with the summer weather
> Too much grass and too much sleep
> I, their shepherd, sing to thee
>   That summer is a joy to me ...

It was a deeply touching moment for Elizabeth as well as for her aunt, a moment of complete belonging, at the edge of the separation that would come if she married Robbie. It was also to be the only moment of unselfconscious intimacy on her wedding day. Walking, just after dawn, with her aunt and uncle, was the beginning of what later seemed a hallucination that lasted until the sun went down and the day ended.

The wedding was set for eleven o'clock. By nine, home was like a madhouse. Loud voices were calling for things, children cried, and there was the occasional sound of something falling or breaking. All of this was part of a cheerful noise: the cries, the shouts, the broken glass. One of her uncles passed by her room singing:

Here comes the bride, with the idiot by her side

Another sang 'Bringing in the Sheaves':

Sowing in the sunshine, sowing in the shadows
Fearing neither cloud nor winter's chilling breeze ...

Someone was trying to quell the singing until everyone had gotten dressed and ready. Elizabeth herself was sitting in a chair in her bra and panties while her cousin Lisa helped her put on makeup. At times, it felt as if everything were happening *to* her or *around* her, but, in fact, she was an excited participant, asking for this and that, answering questions, even laughing at times. She celebrated with her cousins and reassured her aunt Anne that everything would be all right. Somewhere inside her she was happy, not about marrying Robbie but about the fact of her family: her relatives as well as her best friends (her bridesmaids), who had come early and were now telling her how beautiful she looked, how beautiful her dress looked, how happy they were.

Somewhere inside herself, Elizabeth was pleased, but she stood slightly apart from her own happiness. At the rehearsal, the wedding had seemed an abstraction or a distant ideal. On this day, the day it should all have felt real, the wedding was still distant and strange and she felt like an actor, not a true participant. She assumed this distance from herself was the result of the doubts she had about marrying Robbie, but there was something else: most of the significant moments in her life were really significant only long after they had happened. Sometime from now, whether she married Robbie or not, this day would be meaningful, she knew it.

The day itself was made for a wedding. The sun was a yellow disk. There were great, fluffy white clouds that looked as though they had been hung with care in the sky. From time to time, a breeze blew, bringing with it the smell of dust and the feel of autumn. It was warm, but it was not so warm that one felt uncomfortable in one's special clothes. Footsteps sounded like percussion precisely, rightly hit. And then, as the limousine her uncle John had hired drove toward Barrow, the countryside that Elizabeth knew intimately watched her as she went by. All was still and bright and much as it would have been in a dream of Barrow.

At eleven o'clock, Elizabeth, her bridesmaids and her uncle John, who was to give her away, stood at the entrance to the church, waiting for their signal to enter. Elizabeth heard the service through the thick doors as if it were mumbled. She was aware of the tension around her. She held on to the train of her dress, the material feeling stiff enough to shatter. She was aware of her uncle's cologne. She was aware of the grain of the wood of the door to the church. One particular knot was oddly precise: perfect circles in perfect circles in perfect circles.

And then, in an instant, time was up. The tall door opened, the beginning of the Allegretto from Beethoven's Sixth Symphony began, and Elizabeth walked down the aisle of the church. The church was full. There seemed not a space left on a pew. The faces of the people before her were indistinct. That is, although she recognized everyone, she was not always sure who was who. There were just too many for her mind to take in. Here and there a detail stuck out: John Harrington's tie was crooked; Betsy Robertson, who had been her homeroom teacher, was wiping her tears with a blue handkerchief; George Bigland was wearing a white turtleneck. This mass of people leaning to get a better look at her, this was her home. It was to these people she belonged and with whom she felt kinship. The church, St.

Mary's, though it was tall and its white painted walls went up and up, felt full to bursting as it held her world.

To one side of the church, the stained-glass windows were especially vivid. Elizabeth noticed them, as if for the first time. She took them in, in their entirety, in the momentary glance she gave them. Abbo of Fleury had a hand raised up to protect himself against a group of men who had poles and torches raised above their heads, the angry mob with terrifying expressions on their faces. Alexis of Rome was solitary, his hand held out for alms while, behind him, the Coliseum stood on a hill. Elizabeth looked up toward the altar and saw Robbie standing there, smiling, Phil Bigland, his best man, stood beside him. And she knew, the instant she saw his face, that she did not love Robert Myers. She *had* loved him, perhaps as recently as moments ago, but she did not love him now and knew it for sure. The girl she had been, the one who had loved a boy named Robbie Myers, had finally died, somewhere in transit between home and church. The woman she was did not feel horror or sadness or, even, indifference. She liked Robert still. He was amusing. He was good for her, in that he sometimes kept her from her own worst thoughts, but one was supposed to marry one's beloved and Robert Myers was not her beloved.

As she approached, she imagined he would see her change of heart in her eyes. They stood, as Father Pennant gave a short sermon on marriage and passages from the Bible were read. Before she knew it, it was time for the vows.

– Dearly beloved, said Father Pennant, we are gathered together here in the presence of God and in the face of this company to join together this man and this woman in holy matrimony, a sacrament held honourable amongst all men and women and so not by any to be entered into unadvisedly or lightly, but reverently, discreetly, advisedly and solemnly.

While wondering which of these adverbs she could commit to – 'discreetly' being the only one with a real chance – her mind drifted and she missed Father Pennant's words, missed being given away by her uncle, and only came around when Robbie took her hand and looked her in the eyes – evidently unaware that she no longer loved him.

– Do you, said Father Pennant, Robert Myers, take Elizabeth Denny to be your wife? Will you love her, comfort her, honour and keep her, in sickness and in health, for richer, for poorer, for better or worse, forsaking all others as long as you both shall live?

– I will, said Robert.

And then, for an instant, time stopped for Elizabeth. She looked, for what seemed hours, into the eyes of Robert Myers. She studied him. She had a memory of them making love for the first time, when they were fourteen. How certain she had been that she loved him and wanted to marry no one else! There were no such feelings now. Not a shred of confidence remained.

Father Pennant finished his part of her vow.

– ... forsaking all others as long as you both shall live?

Elizabeth hesitated and time stretched out. She could not find the right road within her. But then, the thing she was waiting for came: a vision of Barrow, Barrow seen from the air, its houses and farms interlocking. Barrow was hers, its mind her mind. And Robert was part of it all, a part she knew, a part that could not hurt her anymore, because she did not love him. She was immune to his lunacy. The important thing – the *only* thing – was that she wanted to begin her life, here, in this place. So, although she did not love the man, Elizabeth said

– I will.

They exchanged rings. Father Pennant spoke again, facing Robert.

– You may now kiss the bride, he said.

Which Robert did, his lips on hers feeling, to her, like warm, soft rubber, behind which were his teeth. Then, the music sounded and all those in the church rose to applaud. All approved. All were happy, though in the midst of that happiness was Elizabeth herself: bewildered, married to someone she no longer loved, her husband.

The bride and groom, priest and witnesses, retired to the vestry where, on a table, there was the book they were to sign and two lit candles. Robert was ecstatic or, simply, relieved. His grin was unreadable. Someone took a picture as he signed his name in the registry. As Robert signed and as the picture was taken, Elizabeth's attention was drawn by one of the candles. It was nondescript, as far as candles go: six or seven inches tall, three inches in diameter. The flame danced as candle flames will, but Elizabeth was mesmerized by it, by the way it fluttered, the flame itself suggesting something solid and thick. No wonder, she thought, the ancients compared flame to a bird.

Gently, Father Pennant said

– Elizabeth?

– Yes? she answered.

– Your turn to sign the registry.

Robert kissed the side of her head as she signed the book. Then, as suddenly as it had begun, the ceremony was over. Back down the aisle she went, with her arm in Robert's while, outside the church, a crowd waited to cheer and throw rice.

It was odd to be in a field in her wedding dress, but she had agreed to keep the dress on so people could take pictures of the bride. As the reception was in a field at the Biglands', however, a field normally occupied by sheep, she longed to be in something less delicate. Also, given her ambivalence about her husband, she did not want to be in the dress any longer than she had to. It seemed there were hundreds of people with her, dozens who wanted pictures: friends, family, Barrownians, the human parameters of her world.

Everyone seemed genuinely pleased by the wedding they'd witnessed: *her* wedding. She was congratulated, endlessly. Her dress was admired. Her radiance was remarked on. All the while, as if they were now indissociable, Robert stood beside her, holding her hand, kissing her whenever people asked to take a photo. Robert's family was as thrilled as her own. Some had come from as far away as Winnipeg. One of his uncles, the one who had patted her behind, had come from Ocala, Florida.

In all of this, it was difficult for her to figure out what Robert felt about their wedding. Did he realize she did not love him? Did that matter? To break the smile on his face, you would have had to hit it with a hammer. It was possible, wasn't it, that this smile hid his indifference to her? She would have to wait until later to hear what he said. She would know his feelings that night, their wedding night, when they would sleep together as husband and wife for the first time. She did not know how he felt about it, but just about the last thing she wanted from him was sex. They would have to make love at some point, if only to mark the occasion, but she did not know how she would react to his touch. Before this day, she had always – mostly always – enjoyed their lovemaking. It was strange that the very idea should become a problem on the one day when it should have been a consecration of their feelings. But she had married him. She had said yes. She had not stood him up. She had not told the truth about her feelings. Perhaps, now, this feeling of alienation would be the principal one, the one fact of their marriage. For a moment, as she looked at her husband and then at all the smiling people around him, she felt a monumental bitterness, a bitterness so deep it could sweep the world away or, at least, make everything in it unbearable. Her own smile felt like a small hand-kerchief held up before her naked body. Almost in self-defence, she took her husband's hand and kissed his lips. The people around them laughed. Mr. Bigland said

– Save it for the motel.

Could he really be drunk so soon?

Her wedding was what gossipmongers would call a lavish occasion. The food was still being cooked and put on the long tables. It seemed everyone in Barrow had contributed something. There was more gelatin, more flavours and varieties of gelatin, than you could easily keep in memory: red gelatin with bits of slaw and carrots suspended within, a yellow gelatin with pineapple pieces, an orange one in which something was suspended like smoke in a small sunlit room. There were pots of potato salad with its yellowish mayonnaise and bowls of greens. Beside the tables, at a slight remove, a barbecue pit had been dug. In it a whole pig was roasting, its blackened corpse continually turned and faithfully doused with a barbecue sauce that smelled of molasses, mustard and oranges. Beyond the barbecue, parts of a cow were being cooked and roasted on a black grill from which plumes of smoke rose. Also, there were drinks. Bottles of alcohol: rum, gin, vodka, beer, scotch, rye and, though no one in town liked it much, wine. There was also, of course, champagne and, as almost everyone had had a glass, Elizabeth had one too. It tasted like a fizzy vinaigrette in which someone had dropped sugar and pieces of apple.

Finally, at its own table apart from the others, there was her wedding cake. It was odd to see it here, in a field, beneath a white canopy. It was tall and magnificent. All the affection John Harrington had for her had gone into its making. The details, the florettes and silhouettes, were precisely done. You could smell the marzipan from a distance away, as if the cake were an almond censer. Impressive and elegant, it suggested great love and it was for this reason that, seeing it here, in this still-green field, Elizabeth began to cry. How inadequate and petty her feelings were, compared to the deep feelings Mr. Harrington's patience and kindness were meant to celebrate.

Her aunt Anne was beside her in an instant, holding her hand and wiping the tears from her face, as if Elizabeth were still a child and homeless as she had been at her parents' death. Though she did not want to upset Elizabeth further, her aunt also began to cry, as quietly as she could, overcome by the thought of her child, and in the end Elizabeth *was* her child, leaving, happily married, as she imagined.

– Is everything all right? someone asked.

— Yes, yes, someone else answered. It's tears of joy.

And before Elizabeth knew it, she and her aunt were surrounded by cooing friends, all congratulating her on her happiness.

At some point, Elizabeth imagined she understood the meaning of the day. She and Robert, at the centre of this maelstrom, were being made to feel the magnitude of all this, the wedding and the reception. And it suddenly occurred to her that a wedding was like a train wreck or an inner-city mugging, a fall from a survivable height or a near drowning. It was a trauma that would — that was *meant to* — bring them closer.

After the meal, Elizabeth had at last gone in to change her clothes. Her suitcases were packed. She and Robert were off to England, to the Lake District, where Robert's family had come from three hundred years previously. Some of Elizabeth's people had also been English and had come from a place in Suffolk (mythic, in her imagination) called Snape. But her English relatives, once they reached the New World, had intermingled and intermarried, so that Elizabeth was more French Canadian or Native Canadian than she was anything else.

After changing clothes, Elizabeth and Robert danced for the guests. They danced in the field, as the embers used to cook the pig darkened to black. For the bride and groom's final dance, the band from Glencoe played something that sounded Celtic. And it pleased her to dance. There was meaning to all this too: the association of man and woman in dancing was itself a kind of matrimony, two and two, a necessary conjunction, holding each other by the hand or the arm in concord. For a moment, dancing with Robert, she was happy. Not that she suddenly loved him, but she liked him, because he did not mind dancing, because he was not a wilfully cruel man, because he loved his family and because, in the end, she believed he loved her. And because she was happy, she stopped worrying about their future.

Around six o'clock, the newlyweds were ready to leave. Their time together as husband and wife had begun. Elizabeth wanted a last look at the land that was home, before she left for Pearson Airport in Toronto, so she quietly walked away while Robert said goodbye to his friends. Somehow, a few of the sheep had strayed from their pen. They stood eating grass at the periphery of her wedding, as if curious about the goings-on, but not too curious. They kept their distance. Elizabeth walked toward them, away from the reception, unobstructed now that she was in normal clothes. The sheep were so used to humans, they scarcely reacted to her approach: a little bleating, a shifting, as if to make room for her, and then they were quiet, thoughtfully eating the grass and weeds.

As she passed them, it struck Elizabeth that she had always loved sheep, but she had rarely paid much attention to them. They were, simply, a part of her world. She stopped, turned back and stood looking at the sheep for a while: dirty fleeces, fat-looking flanks, delicate legs, almost invisible tails, the smell of them, the weight of them in the mind so different from the weight of cows, say, or dogs. In her imagination, it was as if one could pick a sheep up with one hand, like raising a cloud. Not true, of course, not true. They were beautiful and solid and having taken their beauty in, Elizabeth walked on toward a rise in the land from which one could see all the way to Barrow, its houses.

Elizabeth was alone for no more than a few minutes before Father Pennant approached.

– It's beautiful, he said. Isn't it?

Elizabeth looked out over southern Ontario, the land beneath them, oddly misshapen squares of dark green, black and yellow. Here and there were farmhouses and barns. To one side, there were the woods. And beyond, the crab shape of a small town: Barrow. This was who she was. Had her parents lived, her destiny might have been different. She might have had these feelings for Strathroy or Ottawa, Windsor or Thunder Bay. But her parents had died and this was the place that had taken her in, and she could imagine, finally, that in death the land would take her broken body and care for it as it would for all bodies that had walked the earth.

– Yes, she answered. It is beautiful.

– Sometimes, said Father Pennant, I think it's all we have.

– I don't think it's *all* we have, Father.

– You're right, said Father Pennant immediately. You're right. There's more. Are you enjoying your wedding?

– It feels a little strange to call it enjoyable.

Father Pennant laughed.

– I find weddings strange too, he said. No ... mysterious is a better word. They're mysterious. All the sacraments are, when you think of it. They're moments when the grace of God touches the earth. I mean, that's what the Church teaches.

– You don't believe that? asked Elizabeth.

– Yes, yes, of course I do. But it's still mysterious, however you describe it. I mean, you don't have to bring God into it. The very idea that two people choose to get married in the first place is mystery enough.

– Yes, said Elizabeth. It is mysterious.

They spoke for a few more minutes, before Father Pennant wished her a happy honeymoon. He was going to walk to Barrow, to work off some of the wonderful food he'd eaten.

– It's one of the finest weddings I've been to, he said.

He walked away, wishing her all the best in the life to come with her husband and – did they want children? – children.

Elizabeth stood alone for a moment longer, thinking of Father Pennant's words about the world being all we have. Well, if that was true, if the land was all – no God, no love, no others – she could still be happy because, in the end, everything came from the land, from the smallest thing to, maybe, God Himself. Anything you took away, the land would give back. Or so it felt to her, at that moment, and she walked back to the reception, tired and content.

Yes, she did want children.

The next day, the very next day, the new life would begin in earnest. It would have its problems, of course. She was not certain she could remain married to Robert Myers, that she would be Mrs. Myers for long. But she put her doubts aside as she returned to the field and to her various families.

Father Pennant went on his way back to Barrow. He passed through the woods, its darkness a little intimidating, before coming out by the highway that looked down onto Barrow. His thoughts were confused. Had he really asked Elizabeth Denny if she didn't feel Nature was all? He should not have. (Nor should he have had the feelings he fleetingly felt for her. For the briefest of moments, as he asked Elizabeth about children, he had imagined the salt taste of her, the feel of her tongue on his, the animal *there*-ness of her body.)

Since the death of Lowther Williams, he had become so passionate about his study of the land around Barrow that he sometimes lost sight of the world beyond, of God the creator. Even now, at the thought of 'God the creator,' he felt an unexpected twinge of mistrust. Mistrust? Yes, 'mistrust' was *almost* the word. Take the implications of Lowther's death, the implications of a 'compact' with God. He supposed that some would have taken Lowther's death as a manifestation of God's mercy or, at very least, His will. That is, *if* they accepted that God had interrupted His infinite discretion to kill Lowther himself. For a while, he'd preferred to think of Lowther's death as a coincidence – perhaps, even, an unconsciously made decision on Lowther's part, a suicide carried out unawares. Now, however, he admitted to himself that, yes, it was possible for the infinite to concern itself with the death of a being. Perhaps it was even right. Perhaps if Lowther or any of his male antecedents had lived beyond the age of sixty-three, there would have been catastrophic consequences. So, Lowther's death had been justified. But if so, that made any 'god' who carried out the execution a caretaker, a gardener pulling weeds. And as it was with Lowther, so it was with loaves and fishes and the parting of the Red Sea. God, ultimately, was useful. But why call Him 'creator'? Why should we say God created Nature rather than, as the ancient Greeks believed, Nature created the gods, that 'god' was subject to Nature's laws and interdictions? It was easier to believe, easier for him to believe, anyway, in the rules of Nature binding God rather than the other way around.

Honestly, that sheep couldn't have done better if it *had* been divine.

Christopher Pennant knew, or felt, that his thinking was suspect, but he could do nothing about his thoughts. He was again experiencing the struggle for faith he'd experienced as a seminarian. And, yet, he was not unhappy. More than that: as he walked home he was in the very best of moods, as joyful as if a storm had passed and the world was restored to its entrancing self. The early evening sun was still bright, though the clouds in the distance were reddish and darkening. The air was clean and smelled of the woods, of the fields, of the world itself over which a light breeze blew.

He thought again of the sheep he'd encountered in Preston's field. He then immediately thought (again) of Lowther and then of Lowther's prayer book. The prayer book, which had once belonged to Lowther's father, had had every prayer crossed out but one. The one prayer left, a perverse prayer for death, had itself been crossed out by Lowther, almost certainly in the days when he had believed God had abandoned him. So, on the dresser in what had been Lowther's room, there was an entirely useless prayer book. Useless? No, not useless. In that it served as a memento of Lowther, Father Pennant could not bring himself to throw it out. There, you see? There was an example of spirit (Lowther's spirit) adhering to a thing (the prayer book). You could use Lowther's prayer book as proof that the world was more than material, couldn't you? No sooner had he asked himself this question, though, than it was dismissed. The only value the book had was in him, Christopher Pennant. It was not in the book itself.

The realm of the spirit was, decidedly, becoming strange to him.

As he walked along the road to Barrow, Christopher Pennant was reminded of the day, some five months gone, when he had walked into town for the first time. He had been entranced by the world around him. He was still entranced, but there was a difference. On this day, he was no longer certain he wanted to remain in Barrow. Five months previously, he had been charmed by this, his first parish. More recently, the thought had come to him that, perhaps, Barrow was not enough. It was as lovely and as interesting as any town could be. Its inhabitants were mainly good people. Its rituals were commonplace, save for those that were not. And the life of the town was almost certainly enough to sustain his interest, at least for a time. But what about the land? The land was wonderful and absorbing, but there were other kinds of plants elsewhere, other moths, other butterflies, other beetles. Having become adept at cataloguing and drawing the world around him, it was natural, wasn't it, that he should be curious about Nature in other places?

There was a partial solution to this dilemma, of course: a greenhouse. Heath had suggested that the one way Lowther did not want his money used was for the construction of a greenhouse, but Christopher Pennant was not convinced Heath was right. After all, as Heath had said, Lowther trusted Christopher's judgment. If Christopher Pennant wanted a greenhouse, why should there not be a greenhouse in Barrow? Priests were always going on about charity, but why not give something deeper: a place where anyone could go to witness the thrilling variety of Nature's gifts? Anyway, he would think about it. There was no need to quickly spend the money he'd been left.

Looking over the land, Christopher Pennant thought of the priests who had preceded him in this country. They had been among the first Europeans to explore Canada. They had come with a mission: to lead the natives to Christianity and salvation. In their single-mindedness, they had done as much harm as good, poor men. They would have done better to learn from those who knew the land.

Instead, they had prepared the way for a civilization that had, over the years, turned away from earth, land and ground. He did not identify with the Jesuits but neither did he identify with any specific tribe. Rather, he envied the ones – whoever they might have been – who'd come through this part of the world when it was virginal.

As he walked into Barrow, somewhere around seven o'clock, evening was in the early stages of suffusion. The world was not yet dark. It was beautiful: a hint of winter in the air, the lights of the town coming on as its inhabitants, each in his or her own time, became aware of the coming darkness.

London, England, 2009
Quincunx 1

Typeset in Albertan and Gotham.

Albertan was designed by the late Jim Rimmer of New Westminster, B.C, in 1982. He drew and cut the type in metal at the 16pt size in roman only; it was intended for use only at his Pie Tree Press. He drew the italic in 1985, designing it with a narrow fit and a very slight incline, and created a digital version. The family was completed in 2005 when Rimmer redrew the bold weight and called it Albertan Black. The letterforms of this type family have an old-style character, with Rimmer's own calligraphic hand in evidence, especially in the italic.

Printed at the old Coach House on bpNichol Lane in Toronto, Ontario, on Zephyr Antique Laid paper, which was manufactured, acid-free, in Saint-Jérôme, Quebec, from second-growth forests. This book was printed with vegetable-based ink on a 1965 Heidelberg KORD offset litho press. Its pages were folded on a Baumfolder, gathered by hand, bound on a Sulby Auto-Minabinda and trimmed on a Polar single-knife cutter.

Edited and designed by Alana Wilcox
Cover design by Ingrid Paulson and Alana Wilcox
Cover painting A Lady Sheep, by Lindee Climo, courtesy of the artist and the Mira
    Godard Gallery. From the collection of the Dufferin County Museum and
    Archives, as photographed by Pete Paterson.

Coach House Books
80 bpNichol Lane
Toronto ON M5S 3J4
Canada

416 979 2217
800 367 6360

mail@chbooks.com
www.chbooks.com

ABOUT THE AUTHOR

André Alexis was born in Trinidad and grew up in Canada. His debut novel, *Childhood*, won the Books in Canada First Novel Award, the Trillium Book Award, and was shortlisted for the Giller Prize and the Writers' Trust Fiction Prize. His previous books include *Asylum*, *Beauty and Sadness* and *Ingrid and the Wolf*.

A NOTE ON THE TEXT

Pastoral is, in part, an homage to Beethoven's Sixth Symphony, the *Pastoral* Symphony. The novel's chapters follow the logic of the symphony whose five movements are entitled:

1. Awakening of cheerful feelings upon arrival in the country
2. Scene at the brook
3. Happy gathering of country folk
4. Thunderstorm; Storm
5. Shepherds' song; cheerful and thankful feelings after the storm

The *Pastoral* Symphony is also inextricably associated – in my mind – with Lambton County, where I grew up. This novel is, thus, a paean to the place where I first learned what Nature was to mean for my Canadian self.